The Lost Tribe of Eden

The Lost Tribe of Eden

March of the Boneface

BY

JOSHUA LEE FARLEY

ISBN: 9798680375136

THE DAYS BEFORE

PROLOGUE

As Benjamin sat beside the fire, he heard for the first time the story of how the people had come to know the ways of the wolf the eagle and the ways of the men of violence. He sat in silence as one of the old ones told the story of his people in the language of the first man. The true language of all men.

It was the story of how the first warrior had come to be, as well as how his daughter, the Blackbird, had come to be known as the greatest of all warriors.

The people had once fallen from Eden. They had also, through the sacrifice of one of their own, found their way back. As the light of the fire shone on the face of the old one, Benjamin could see his many wrinkles, and it looked as if all the wisdom of life were held somewhere deep behind them.

What the old one had said were things that Benjamin had not expected to hear—not only because of what had taken place so long ago but also because it had so much meaning for the people today. The old one had said to all who were there, along with all who would ever hear these words from the mouths of future generations, that this place where they were now, had always been the people's home.

"Remember," he said, reminding them all that they were no more than a lie away from losing the truest of all things. He reminded them that those things could not be seen with one's eyes.

"Remember!" the old one said as he stood up from where he sat, looking at them all as the light danced across their faces. This is what Benjamin heard that night in the light of the fire, the very same fire that had cast its light on the Warrior, as well as the Blackbird, so long ago. This was long before the first war cries had ever fallen on the ears of the people.

"Come sit and hear the words of our ancestors," the old one said as he motioned all to gather around.

"When we were still in the land of our people, it provided us with all that we needed so that we had never known what it was to want. We lived in peace with all men.

"We knew the ways of the bear, the wolf, and the turtle. We were one, and one was us. All was as it had always been, good. This was all in the days of our ancestors—the 'days before,' as they are known to us."

The old one's hands raised into the air, then he made a sweeping motion that was meant to show that all those that were there were included. He brought both hands to his chest, hitting it as his eyes moved to each one of them until he had the attention of them all.

"Who are the people?" he asked as he brought his hands back down to his side. "Let me tell you the story of who the people are. Listen to the wind; it knows," he said raising one hand into the air as if he were taking hold of it as it passed, leading them all to another time. Ask the trees; they'll tell you. The old one's eyes peering through the night at the old oak tree that was set off a short ways behind them all, giving a nod as if it were an old friend. "The rocks all know the story of the ones known as the people. Do you want to know how?" he said as his eyes fell on Benjamin for a moment. "The same way all things know." He stopped as he took in a deep breath. "The Creator told them, he's telling you all now." The old one reached down, grabbing a piece of wood and throwing it into the fire, causing sparks to fly up and into the air.

"Who are the people?" Again waiting a brief moment before speaking. "You are the people, and not just you. Oh no, all men who call this world home are the people. It was created for men and not one man more than another. These are the words from the days before.

The men would hunt, bringing back all types of game. With love in their hearts, the women prepared the meals for all. The village was set in a small valley between two large mountains, having a high mountain pass leading into this paradise. There were streams teeming with fish, as well as long grasses of many types. Wildflowers, songbirds, as well as acorns and honey. There was nothing more they could want. This was considered the center of all known creation.

"As time passed the people had grown in number, so that some of their children began to gather further and further from where their parents as well as their grandparents had been raised up. It did not matter; all knew that it was this place that all men's ancestors had come from.

So, if a man should come upon another man that he did not know as he walked along the trail, it did not matter. Both were one of the people, just as all men were. They would extend their hands to one another and say, 'Hello brother,' and all would be good.

Soon the people had grown so greatly in number that their homes pushed out onto the river. "One day as some children played, they saw a viper on the shore of the opposite side of the river. This was a place that was forbidden, but as children are sometimes curious, they watched as the viper drank.

"The viper, being a cunning and devious creature, could see that the children were interested in him and also that they were able to grab hold of things. He thought to himself how nice it would be to have a home built for him, instead of having to crawl into the cracks of rocks. That's when he decided to hide from the people so that he was not seen for a very long time.

"One day, after those children were grown, one of them said to himself, 'Why not put my home on the other side of the river? I have not seen a viper for so long, that I doubt that they are even around anymore. I will be the first one of the people to do this.'

"Despite food being scarce on the other side of the river, that is what the man decided to do.

"One by one, some of the people started to follow until many of them were on that side of the river. Every day they would cross over to gather food and return to their homes in the evening. This was all before the day of the Great Storm, as it was known.

"Once the Great Storm fell upon the land, and once all the ice had finally begun to melt, the river had become so deep and so wide that the people could not see from one side to the other. It had been so long since the people had been able to cross that not even one person could say that they had ever seen a man from the other side of the river.

"One day in summer, as a boy climbed atop a tall tree, he began to shout to the others down below. 'Come look!'" he shouted. 'I can see the other side of the river.'

'Get down!' The boy's father said as he rushed to the bottom of the tree, looking up. His son, sitting high above in the tree's branches, was staring out in the direction of the sun.

"'I said, get down!' the man repeated, pulling his hands up as he tried to block the sun's rays from his eyes.

"'Father, come see the other side of the river!' said the boy as he continued to shout to the others, still not turning away from where he was looking.

'Get down son!' the man shouted again, but the boy would not, and as the night fell, the man was forced to climb up to get the boy. From high up in the tree's branches he also first saw the other side of the river.

"'It's true; I see it!' the man shouted down to the others.

"Excitement could be seen on the faces of all the people. They all knew the stories that were told to them about their brothers that had lived in the land of rock and thorn, lost to time and distance. This was all during the days before.

"Day by day the waters receded, and in time the people saw their brothers from the other side of the river again.

"These men came across the river on small wooden villages

that were pulled by the wind as they floated on the surface of the water. Not only had these men changed in appearance, but since they had been gone so long, they had also changed in their ways.

"The people offered many gifts to their brothers, but their brothers offered none. The visitors also took things that were not offered. Two girls had been invited to the ones with eyes of the sky's floating village, but when the girls' father asked to have them returned, the visitors struck him, and the girls were never seen again. Because of this, a great sadness took hold of the people, and the next time the visitors from across the river came, the people would not greet them. They would not see another man from the other side of the river again until the one known as the Soldier was found on its shore many years later. He would be the father of the tribe's medicine man."

CHAPTER 1

Sutkey and Teeosh were both beautiful young ladies of the tribe with long black hair and big brown eyes. Sutkey had a pleasant way about her, and the tribe was proud of the woman she had grown to be.

Teeosh had a less pleasant way as she was quick to avoid her chores. It was in an attempt to avoid her work that many had said was the beginning of the end of the days before.

One day, as the girls were busy working down by the river, grinding acorns into a thick paste that was used in many of the tribe's favorite meals, Sutkey noticed that Teeosh was nowhere in sight. At first Sutkey thought that her sister was trying to get out of her chores by hiding in the woods. This was something that she had done many times, so Sutkey was not surprised by this. After most of the day had passed, there was still no sign of Teeosh, and her sister began to worry, having a feeling that something was wrong. Soon all were on the river bank at the very spot that Teeosh's footprints had led them to.

"Teeosh! Teeosh!" The people all called for the rest of that day and well into the night, but with no answer, many had begun to lose hope. Some feared that the fast-moving current had taken her, while others believed that an evil spirit had led her to her doom.

The next morning her footprints were discovered on the opposite side of the river, continuing deep into the land. With no hope of following her because of the many dangers, once again a great sadness took hold of the people.

With Teeosh gone, the seasons came and went, and it felt like it had been so long that even Sutkey had begun to believe that she would never see her sister again.

One day, as she sat down at the very spot where she had last seen her sister's footprints, she heard someone crying. The sound seemed to be coming from the other side of the river.

"Hello? Is there anyone there?" shouted Sutkey, but there was no answer. Then up from behind a rock came the eyes of a boy!

"Hello? Are you OK?" asked Sutkey as she tried to remain calm.

The eyes slowly began to rise so that the boy could be seen.

"Are you OK?" Sutkey asked again in a calm voice so that she would not frighten the boy. Still there was no answer, but the boy started to point at the ground behind the rocks. "It's OK. I'm going to get help," she said as she turned back to the village, running as fast as her feet could carry her. "This way," Sutkey said as she urged the hunters to follow her to where the little boy had been. Once they reached the spot where she had seen him, there he was, just like she had said.

Reaching the bank of the river, the hunters jumped into the water and began to swim across to the other side. Once they came to the rocky shore, they could see just what the boy had been pointing at. One of the hunters reached down, and when he came back up from behind the rock, it was Teeosh that he held in his arms.

It had been a long journey with the boy, and Teeosh had given all she had to make it back to the river and her people.

The people laughed and smiled, and there were hugs for all as a much-needed celebration had begun.

"What happened to you sister? Where did you go?" Sutkey asked.

"OK, all that in time, but first, I want you to meet someone," said Teeosh as she looked to where all the people stood. From behind them all, out came the boy. Since he looked different from any child that Sutkey had ever seen, she was surprised at what she heard next.

"Sister, that little boy standing in front of you is Drone. Drone is my son," said Teeosh. All the people were looking on as the two sisters shared the moment.

"Your son? But how? He looks like the ones from the land of rock and thorn, only smaller, of course." This was true—Drone did have the eyes of the sky as well as hair like the sun. This was how the people had remembered the Soldier, who was the Medicine Man's father.

"His father is the one known as the Commander, who is also a son of the Soldier, the Medicine Man's father." Teeosh knew that this was the first time that the people had heard of the Medicine Man's half-brother from the other side of the river.

"Come Drone, say hello to my sister, Sutkey" said Teeosh as she tried to wave the boy over. Teeosh was hoping to give her sister a better look at him, but Drone refused to come any closer.

"It's OK. I don't bite," Sutkey said, trying to assure Drone that it was safe.

"Maybe not, but he might," Teeosh said with a half-hearted laugh. She could feel the eyes of the Medicine Man on her and she knew why.

"Maybe later," said Sutkey, smiling at the boy.

"Teeosh, what happened to you that day? Where did you go?"

"I'm sorry sister; I was foolish, and just didn't want to do my work. I waited until I could see that you were busy. That's when I crossed over to the other side of the river. Once I was there, I just kept on walking until I couldn't remember my way back. It must have been days before I couldn't stand anymore, so I just lay there and waited to die. The next thing I remember, I was lying across the back of a horse in a long line of horses." Sutkey could hardly believe what she was hearing. "where did they take you Teeosh?"

"To the ones with eyes of the sky's village, where I was brought to a large stone dwelling that was built on top of a low hill. This was the home of Drone's father. His home was a fortress, built for the purpose of defending themselves in case of war." Teeosh's eyes were fixed into a distant gaze, remembering the day she had first felt fear.

"What is war" asked Sutkey. She had never heard this word.

"War was something that would happen when the sickness became so bad that it could not be controlled. When this would happen, the people would all gather with their weapons in hand. Then, they would all go out and do murder. This was mostly the men, but some women too were part of this war."

Teeosh continued to tell of the things that had happened to her and of the sickness.

"Why would they take part in this war? Sutkey asked.

Teeosh said that there were many different reasons. "They were scared and believed that they had no choice, or that they would profit from it. Some even believed that it was necessary, but whatever the reason, the people have never had the need for murder, and we have always had all that we could not only need but also want. That is how I know that it is a sickness and not something that is necessary." Sutkey could only listen as she tried to understand her sisters words.

"This is how a few would get the rest to participate in war. It was for the purpose of taking things that did not belong to them and so by their own words say that those things did belong to them now. They never had to take it because none of this is ours for them to take it from. We live here together." Teeosh continued explaining to her sister what had happened to her. "They would use these reasons to be angry, and so murder. They murdered so that they could say all that could be seen with ones eyes was theirs, and none would say different. They did not know that the truest of all things cannot be seen with one's eyes. So, they made a word and called it 'to *own*.'

"How can this be? Does the mother have say over the child when the child is a man? If this were true, then what would the man do when the mother went on and left this world? That is what these people do not know. That *own* is a lie. The man does as his mother says because she gave him love, not because he is owned."

The Commander oversaw many men who looked to him

for his say on what they would do for every moment of the day.

"When the Commander's men first brought me to him, I was very scared, but since his men had saved my life, I hoped that he would be as kind. I soon found out that I was very wrong."

Teeosh could recall all that he had said on that day.

■ ■ ■

"So my child" the Commander said as he began to stand. The space was dimly lit, but Teeosh could make out the silhouettes of soldiers sitting in the shadows. "I can see that you are from one of the tribes on the other side of the river," he continued with a look of annoyance at the sight of her. His eyes were cold, with no kindness in them. The Commander's men all turned their heads to look at the girl. Suddenly, a feeling of fear came over her, and she wished that she were any place but where she was.

"I am" she answered. "Could you show me the way back to the river so that I may return to my people?" she continued, taking in a deep breath. The Commander had no reaction as he just looked at her, and for a moment she wondered if she had even spoken out loud.

One by one the Commander's men began to stand, until they were all looking down at her. Teeosh had never imagined that men could be so large, every one of them towering over her. She could see that these men also seemed to have no kindness in them. Certainly showing it was something they could not do. Suddenly home seemed so very far away. She began to wonder if this was even the same world that held Eden on the other side of the river.

As she looked on at these men of iron, she noticed that there in the small spaces, their armor held the dried blood of the men they had killed. It darkened the shiny metal everywhere.

"Now why would I do something like that?" the Commander finally said. His eyes looking into her, tearing down any hope that she would be OK.

"Do you think that my men and I have nothing better to do than spend our time bringing you home?"

His eagerness to strike her became visible and for a moment Teeosh thought that she had seen a young boy appear there on his face.

In the next moment, her head led the rest of her body into a slow turn. Her knees lost the strength to hold her up as her body began to float into nowhere, delivering her into the Commander's hate.

The Commander looked over at the table where he and his men had been going over their tactics of war. A meeting place where they made the plans they would unleash on the weak, wherever they found them.

"I didn't know what to say, so I said nothing. This was something that the Commander would not have." Teeosh continued to recall the events of that day.

"Do you think that I speak only to hear my own voice?" His eyes seemed to turn as black as the soot that covered the homes in the town below.

"That's when he began to put his hands to me as he let his

anger overtake him." Teeosh could see her sister's surprise at hearing all of this.

"So I offered myself to him so that he would stop. This is how Drone came to be."

"I'm sorry sister. I don't know what to say except from that came a wonderful son."

"You're right, but maybe I shouldn't have brought him here to the people. Maybe…. I should have left him with his father, on the other side of the river."

Teeosh confessed this to her sister even though it hurt her very much to do so.

"Why would you say this, Teeosh?" Sutkey wanted to know why her sister would say something so harsh.

"Because of the way his father's people live. It is a way that I still cannot understand."

It was true—the ones on the other side of the river lived in a very different way than the people. Teeosh had wondered if bringing Drone to the peoples home would be safe for the rest of the tribe.

"What are you talking about?" asked Sutkey. She couldn't understand what harm a boy could cause.

"It was a sickness, something that overtook them. When this would happen, they would become like beasts. They would begin to run, many at once, grabbing up a man, and then tearing him to pieces. They would hang the pieces from a tree for all to see. They would also bring their children out to throw rocks at these men before they were *murdered*. They would all cheer, as they seemed to never get enough of this. That is why I don't know if it was right to bring my son here to the people." Teeosh said these things with worry in her spirit. She just hoped that she had not made a mistake.

The two sisters understood that this sickness would destroy the people, so they could only hope to never know it.

CHAPTER 2

Drone was not a kind child. He had taken up many of his father's peoples ways. He would take as he pleased, causing many to avoid him. They would also speak in hushed tones when ever they spoke of the boy .

As he grew, a fear of him also grew because of his temper and his quickness to use his size to achieve his way. Drone stood taller than any other man in the village when he was still a boy of just twelve years old. He soon became aware of the power he had over the rest of the people, using his size to rule over any he chose. He would order others so that he was served first, as well as taking things that did not belong to him.

One day, as the Medicine Man was performing a cleansing ceremony, Drone attempted to grab a sacred rattle from his hand. The Medicine Man quickly took hold of Drone's arm, pulling it up toward the sky, while at the same time kicking Drones feet out from under him, dropping him to the ground.

"You will learn someday to have respect for others," he said as the people looked on.

Drone looked around at the ones who were there, seeing that they all seemed pleased with what the Medicine Man had done.

"What are you looking at?" Drone yelled as he lay on the ground, his eyes filled with rage.

"It's not that we wish harm on you boy. The Medicine Man only wishes to teach you in the ways of the people, in the ways of our ancestors," an old woman said.

"In the ways of *"YOUR" ancestors!*" Drone yelled. The people all could see his anger as he spoke these words. Drone was left with no choice but to stay down and accept defeat. Hatred for the Medicine Man began to burn in his heart from that day on.

One day, as one of the women came upon Drone taking more than his share of the dried meat that was stored at the back of the village, she asked, "What is it that you are doing?"

"Keep your eyes to yourself, and tell your words to follow them!" said Drone as he began to pack a large sack with the meat.

"It is no doubt because your father is not here to discipline you," she continued.

At that moment in anger, Drone took up a large rock, killing the woman. This was in the sight of many children, as well as the Medicine Man.

"*Stop!* What are you doing?" yelled the Medicine Man as he rushed in to help the woman, but he was too late.

The woman lay dead with a terrible wound to her head.

"What's wrong with you? Kick dirt on her, and step over if you need to get by" said Drone as he continued to stuff his sack with the meat. "Come help me, I mean to kill wolves to-night," he continued.

The day after the people had buried the woman, the victim

of the tribe's first murder, they seemed like a swarm of bees that couldn't find their way home. The people were walking from here to there without purpose or direction, their faces empty, pulled down with great sorrow.

They had always cared for one another. Now there was a great emptiness that could never be filled. Not only this, there was a new feeling that caused a numbness in them all. *Fear!*

What could the people do? The boy was without remorse or regret. All felt it was only a matter of time before he would kill again. The people gathered so that they could speak on this matter. It was decided that Drone must leave. Return to the place from which he had come.

"Something must be done," said one of the people speaking on the matter of Drone.

"If we wait any longer, the sickness could spread—if it has not already."

"Yes, I agree," the Medicine Man said since he was familiar with the sickness and the effects of it on any who were in its presence.

Teeosh, also in fear of her son, felt that it was the only choice for the people. The next morning Teeosh, Drone, and the Medicine Man prepared for the long journey.

"I am sorry my son, what you have done is more than the people can accept." Teeosh said to Drone as her tears fell. It was early and still dark outside. Both Teeosh and the Medicine Man had hoped to leave before any of the people awoke.

"Mother! The woman's words were always in my ear day and night, so that I had no peace. I only wish I had done this sooner. My father would have never allowed her to speak to me unless she wished to have her head taken from her shoulders. At least she still has her head so that when she reaches the next, she may be in the ears of the ones who have passed; then they too will know why I did this."

"Enough of this talk. The words that you speak are spoken with the forked tongue of a viper," Teeosh said, hoping that none of the other people had heard what Drone had said.

"If my tongue is forked, it suits me better than the tongue of a mouse, squeaking and hoping not to be eaten by the snake. All know that when the snake strikes, it's too late."

After much time both the Medicine Man and Teeosh returned to the village. Life seemed to go by more slowly than it ever had before with the memories of what Drone had done lingering long after in the peoples minds. Suddenly the sounds of women screaming could be heard in the early evening air as a young mother came running to the others. She held a child in her arms. It seemed that one of the children having seen the murder that Drone had committed, hit another child almost taking another life.

"Something must be done!" yelled a woman. "We've been infected with the Soldier's murder! With that came the fear."

The people decided there would be a protector. So was born the first warrior.

The people would give up one of the children so that a Warrior could be, him being the offering the tribe would allow. A protector to all. Sutkey would be the one asked to make the sacrifice since it was her sister who had brought the sickness into the land.

As both the Medicine Man and Sutkey sat around the fire, he began to speak.

"I know that what I am asking of you is hard. Make your decision only after great consideration. It is your choice to make, yours alone."

Sutkey took a moment before she spoke. Then she looked at the Medicine Man, choosing her words carefully.

"I have accepted that this child is no longer just mine; he is to be the protector of all the people." As she continued to speak, the Medicine Man could hear in her the strength of the people in every one of her words.

"Even though it is a hard choice, it is not mine to make. This has already been decided by the Creator. So please understand when I say I need no more time then now to say yes. I only hope the people are able to allow him to live his destiny." She continued as she took in a slow, deep breath, looking up into nowhere. "My pain is all our pain; it is something that is necessary so that we can hold on to us. Without us, our way will be lost forever."

The Medicine Man understood that her words and her strength were both true as well as brave. This was a moment that the Medicine Man would look back on many times in the years ahead. It was in these times, as he trained the boy, that he would question his decision concerning the boy's purpose for being. That's when those reasons became hard to understand.

Sutkey continued to speak, hoping that the Medicine Man understood why she was saying these words.

"Our children deserve to call Eden home, so our wrongs must be made right; a payment will be paid," said Sutkey as she took in another deep breath, looking out at this place she had come to know as her home. "I have always loved this time of year," she said, staring out into the forest.

The bright reds and deep greens of the trees stood out against the blue sky. Soft clouds held still as if painted there high above the village, creating the perfect view for that very moment.

"The way the leaves change colors. Like nature is reminding us all that life never stays the same. It's just moments held by us in our own memories."

■ ■ ■

As the time came near for the child to be born, the people prepared. They picked a spot in the center of the village where they <u>built</u> a cage-like room of wood and stone that was to be his home. The people had chosen the center of the village so that it would remind them all of the sacrifice that was there, just behind those stone walls.

The Medicine Man would prepare the child; no one else was to have any contact with him, not even his mother.

As the day came close for the warrior to be born, Sutkey made a request of the Medicine Man.

"When the child is born and he is finally in your arms, please take him at once so that I don't see him. Even if I am his mother, I will not be known by him, so I can't have the memories of his face there to haunt me."

Once the child was born, hot sticks were placed into his ears so that he would never hear a woman's voice. A woman's voice was thought to provoke sweet feelings of care and nurturing, therefore causing weakness. The people were instructed to never look at him. It was believed that it would make them familiar, also causing weakness.

At age five he was denied warmth, along with his legs or arms being bound. This would teach him to overcome and to be skilled with both hands and feet.

At age seven he was given his only friend, a small turtle. This was to prepare him for what would be next, the painful process in which the largest turtle shells were cut and shaped so that they could serve as his armor, protecting him on the battlefield. They were also to hide the signs of power that were to be branded into his flesh. These were believed to invoke the powers of those who had passed, along with the signs of the four seasons and most important of all, the sign of *us*—the sign of his people's love.

The Warrior was tied to a log; he hugged it so that his back was exposed. Stones had been shaped into the tribe's sacred signs of power. They were allowed to sit in hot coals until they glowed bright red. The boy shifted as he tried to prepare for them, having no idea of the pain he would be forced to endure.

"Hold still boy. Know that this armor is to protect you so that when the day comes for you to be called upon, you will have all the help that can be given to you."

The sacred signs were meant to produce a love so deep in his heart that it would carry him through the moments when his own strength could not. The symbol that was a sign of his people's love was touched by all of the people and then placed directly over his heart. The mark of *us*.

The Warrior cried—not only then, but at every sign and every turtle shell plate that was in pain made a part of him.

As he lay that night with his skin in a burning torment, having only his dear friend Turtle there to comfort him, he did not sleep, and at sunrise the next morning, they continued the process. He did not cry this time because he had no more tears to cry.

All of these practices were believed to be preparing the boy with the tools he would need to have, so that he would know victory on the battlefield.

Once the armor was complete, the Medicine Man carried the Warrior back to his home. He did not wake for two more days, his body broken and limp.

Next, his food would be placed just out of reach; he was given a sharpened stick with a leather cord attached to the end. Every day his food was placed just a little further away than before until he was very skillful with the spear.

He undertook similar practices with the bow and stone knife, along with several types of slashing weapons, until he had mastered them all.

Then one day, just like before, his food was set just out of reach, but he was left without a way to retrieve it. With nothing the boy waited on the medicine man to offer him a way to reach his food but nothing was offered. After the usual time was given to the boy to finish his meal the food was removed. The boy did not understand as his training continued. Once they had trained for most of the day again his meal was brought but he was given no way to retrieve it, just like before. Again he was given the usual time but he still had not eaten. The warrior seen that his food was about to be taken away and he could not understand why. The medicine man offered no explanation and this caused a desperate anger to begin to grow in the boy. That was when the Medicine Man gave him his power. These were ancient powers believed to have once been used by the one that first subdued the world, before men or creatures called it home. To have the strength of the bear or the reflexes of a cat. To possess the speed of the deer or to take flight like the eagle. One power to be held by its conjurer so that he would wield it against his enemies.

The Medicine Man presented still water; beside it he slammed his foot to the ground. Small ripples appeared on the surface of the water from the impact.

This was how he learned to summon his power. As the Warrior walked, his turtle-shell armor would vibrate in a low tone as he shook his shoulders back and forth. He would use this to invoke the destructive force that was his power, the

Warrior being the center of a wave of destruction. His power being the results of his own pain brought forth in the form of that wave.

All who were within its reach would be at once thrown to the ground in pain, having their eardrums burst from the pressure of the wave.

As the wave moved away from its center, it was mysteriously called back to the place from which it had come in a violent rush of destruction. As the warrior grew, it was clear to see that even though he could not hear, he would not fall short in his ability to do what his purpose was, to protect his people.

His swiftness was unmatched by even the deer. He was able to move as only a blur of a shadow, manipulating his stone knife like a hummingbird's wings in flight. Just the memory of where it had been could be seen.

The seasons came and then left, only to return again; all the while the boy spent his days training with the Medicine Man or alone in his hut in the center of the village with Turtle. This was his entire world, besides what he was able to see while looking out the small holes that he had pushed through his hut's walls. The Warrior would spend his days with the Medicine Man, his training pushing him beyond human limits. The Medicine Man could see that the boy wanted nothing more than to please him.

After a long day of training, doing the many things that would sharpen the Warrior's skills, it would continue well into the night.

"That is good for now. Rest, and we will continue later,"

the Medicine Man said. He could see that the boy's legs were sure to give out from under him at any moment. The Warrior, although tired, did not move from where he stood. He just stared looking at his instructor.

"Are you not tired?" he asked the boy, using his hands.

"I am," the boy answered, also using his hands to speak.

It was their own special language—this is what the Medicine Man had told the young Warrior.

"Then why do you still stand?" He asked, looking at the Warrior, trying to find some sort of answer to what was going on. Even as he looked, the only answer he found was a blank stare without any emotion.

"If I sleep, are you going to leave" asked the boy.

"Leave?" He was not sure what the boy was asking him.

"If you are, I will choose to train," the Warrior motioned with his hands, even though it was difficult for him to do this.

This time the Medicine Man found the answers that he had been looking for, but had hoped he would not find. They seemed to come roaring out from behind the boy's eyes like a river.

The Warrior's eyes were open wide as he stood straight up, looking directly into the eye's of the Medicine Man. This was something that the boy had never done. The two of them had spent many days together, and the Medicine Man realized that it had been a long time since he had seen the warriors face clearly. His head would be looking down toward the ground, with his hair hanging down in his face so that he could never fully be seen.

The Medicine Man could clearly see the boy and he

wondered how long had it been—how had he not noticed that the boy had grown up so much. Suddenly he realized just how lonely the boy was. He was almost desperate for the company of another, and it tore at the Medicine Man's heart to see what he had done.

"No, I will not leave you," he said as the sight of the Warrior was almost more than he could handle. This time it was his eyes that looked to the ground as he was overcome with hurt.

"Rest. I will not leave you," he said with his hands. His strength seemed to be pulled out of him.

"What's wrong?" he asked the boy, still not looking directly at the Warrior. He could feel tears forming in his eyes, and he tried to regain himself.

"What's wrong with you?" asked the boy as he seemed to be looking into the heart of the medicine man.

"Nothing, so sleep if you want, or—"

"Or what?" asked the Warrior as he took a step closer. His movement was direct, and the Medicine Man took a short step backward.

"I know," said the Warrior, his grip on his spear tightening.

"Know what?" asked the Medicine Man. He felt like a child that was being forced to explain himself to his father.

"I know that they can see me," said the boy.

"Who can see you?"

"The rest," the boy answered.

"What made you think that they couldn't see you?"

"They never look at me. Is it because I speak in this way and they do not? Why will you not teach me to speak as they do? If I can learn to do these things with a spear and knife, why can I not learn to speak as they do?"

The Warrior took another step forward, and the Medicine Man could see that indeed he had grown into his armor; it was clearly stressed under the pressure his muscles created beneath it.

"I cannot. You will never be able to speak as they do."

"Does that mean I will never be looked at, that I should be alone for all of my life? If this is true, then when will I leave this world?"

"You are not alone. You have Turtle, and what about me?" the Medicine Man said, hoping to have the boy consider this and give him comfort, even if it was unlikely. The boy was no fool. He had most certainly thought of this, but still the medicine man could think of nothing else to say.

"Turtle yes, but what about you?" replied the Warrior. "I see the others with smiles on their faces. Why do I not do this? I did smile once but only once, and that is what Turtle gave to me." The Medicine Man was caught off guard by the boys questions. He struggled to find the words to the boys question. "Why is it given from others, but from you never? What do you want from me so that you will give me a smile of my own?"

"You want to smile?" asked the Medicine Man as he realized he had never seen the boy do this.

"Why not? I did once, but now I cannot remember how this had happened. I try..." and as he said these words, he attempted to smile, but it looked more like he was in terrible pain.

"But it does not feel the same."

The medicine man understood that he would not be able to explain to the boy everything he had asked, so he just stared at the young warrior.

"I cannot answer these things that you ask, so lie down and sleep. Maybe tomorrow these questions will leave you and we can continue to train."

"OK, tell me this first. Why do I train so much? I do not see the others training, not even once."

"I cannot tell you what you want to know," said the Medicine Man. He knew that his answers were not the truth.

"It's not that I want to know; I *need* to know." The boy's eyes were full of pain that he was demanding to be set free from.

"Just sleep. Let the night speak to you. Maybe you will find your answers while you dream. That is all I can say."

With these words on his mind, the Warrior found sleep, but he did not find the answers he needed so badly. Slowly the boy seemed to lose the light that had once danced in his eyes; it was replaced by a dullness that stopped anything bright from being known. The dullness seemed to be cut from the same stone that formed the mountain that held Eden in its shadow, protecting the home of the people, just like the boy would, on the day he would be known.

CHAPTER 4

As time passed, it was clear to the people that Sutkey was having an agonizing time knowing that her son was only a stone's throw away, but he might as well have been on the moon. The people had been instructed never to look at him. She did not want him to know any weakness. She knew that he would need to be without it, when the day came for him to protect the people. It was hard but she obeyed the instructions. She often could hear the boy being pushed by the Medicine Man. She could hear the boys groans as he tried to please his instructor. When this happened, tears filled her eyes. She would hold herself, hoping that he knew that her love for him was all that was dear to her. Pain seemed to always be there, just beneath the surface.

With her pain becoming more difficult to hide from the rest, her beauty started to fade away, along with her smile. Soon she looked as if she were an old woman, and all knew the reason. There was nothing to say that would change this, so she would never find any comfort from the others.

As she tried to do the things that were necessary in life, her eyes often met theirs, and she could see the pity that they had for her in them. She had once tried to confide in Teeosh, but with Teeosh's own guilt because of what Drone had done, Sutkey could see that her sister was unable to offer any comfort.

Then one night in winter, Teeosh walked from inside her hut, telling the others that she would fetch more wood for the fire, even though there was plenty. Teeosh walked out into the cold, and was not seen again until the next day. She lay beneath the snow just outside the Warrior's hut. It seemed that she had never had the wood on her mind. She held in her hand some beads that Sutkey had given her, as well as a lock of hair that was the color of the sun. She lay curled up outside the door of the Warrior, and that was where she finally found peace. Another price paid for the things she had done—one of many that the people would pay before this age was over.

Now that Teeosh was gone and there were no others to talk to, Sutkey slowly began to fade away from herself. Slowly the effects of the sickness appeared in the people as the fear grew from the seed that was planted so long ago.

■ ■ ■

Without answers, the Warrior turned to his only friend Turtle. They often escaped to a place in the Warrior's head. A place where all would see him, and all would have their own personal gifts of smiles just for him. In this place he spoke freely with others; they touched him as if he were like all the rest. To the Warrior, this place was home, and he hoped to someday return. Eden would be a memory he would choose to forget.

As winter approached, the people were finishing up with

their preparations to move deeper into the forest; where they would be safe from the bitter winds and the large wolf packs that came down from the high country in search of food. As the people prepared to pack up and move the village to their winter home, they gathered up their old and young alike.

The packs until then had always been the biggest concern for the tribe. They were dire wolves—large and many in number. They were known to have an appetite for men and were very skilled when it came to getting their prey. The tribe was always on the lookout for any sign that the pack might be near.

As they were finishing their preparations, a sound from the north told them it was time to move. The howls of the dire wolves on the next range told them that the pack would be at the village by the next morning. The people took up their belongings and prepared to leave when again came the howls of the wolves. Panic could be heard as the pack seemed to be under some type of assault. What could cause a whole pack to panic? Not even the bear would cause such a reaction. The Medicine Man knew of only one thing that could accomplish this, men. The kind of men that killed for sport.

The Medicine Man remembered that many of the soldiers of Drone's father's army were draped in wolves' furs, many with their heads still attached, mouths open, showing razor-sharp fangs. The Medicine Man had wondered if any of the wolves would be able to survive the night at the hands of butchers with only blood on their minds. It was doubtful, and for a moment, a sadness for the wolves rushed over him. Then reality hit him, as if the whole of the mountain had fallen on top of him. The Commander and his men were on the people's side of the river.

■ ■ ■

The Warrior stood alone in the darkness that was also held prisoner by the walls of his hut. It was as if all the light had been squeezed out of this space so that the darkness hummed. The boy stood with his face pressed to the hut's wall so that he could look out the small hole he had pushed through that led to the outside. This was where he had been standing peering out into the darkness. This was his only view of the outside world. It had been for most of his life, and it was something he had done for as long as he could remember. All his fondest memories were set right there in the dark, with his face pressed to the wall. Like the first time he had danced or the first time he had laughed. He could remember it so clearly. The boys had been horse-playing when a dog had run up from out of no-where, pulling one of the boys' pants off, then quickly disap-pearing into the woods. The boy screamed, and they all rolled on the ground with laughter until their sides hurt. He would watch as the people walked from one side of the village to the other, and he hung on every moment. He watched how each one walked and noticed if they ever looked in the direction of his hut. That was always a special moment for the Warrior. He would pretend that they were looking at him. He would play it over and over in his head, and it felt good to be noticed. This was something that always made his day. He would look to turtle so that the moment could be shared with his only friend.

To the boy, it was everything, and he wished for a moment like that now, to get the numbness that roared in his head to stop. The stillness of being alone was his family, a family that he would rather not have. The stillness always seemed to be holding the hands of madness behind its back. It usually came around at this time. It had been dark for awhile, and he could see only a short ways into the night. He really needed to see someone at that moment; it did not matter who. He just needed to not be alone, so he just stood there and waited with his face pressed to the wall. Somehow, just the hope of seeing someone was enough.

"Boy," the Medicine Man called from outside, even if the boy could not hear him. The air that surrounded the hut was always colder than the rest of the night. The boy could see the light of the fire from the torch the Medicine Man carried, but he just stood with his face pressed to the wall.

"Come. I want to show you something." He motioned to the boy to follow him outside, so the boy pulled his face from the hole and walked with his head looking toward the ground to where he was led.

They walked a short ways to a clearing that was off behind the village. There set out for him was some fruit and honey. This was something that the boy loved almost as much as Turtle. As he looked at the Medicine Man's gift, he just stood there. He made no effort to take it as he usually did.

"What's wrong? Don't you want it?" asked the Medicine Man, but no answer came from the boy. The Warrior just stared off into the black.

"Are you OK?" he asked, trying to see the boy's face in the darkness.

"If you want to give me a gift, then give me something that will last forever. Even if I will not be here much longer, what I want will, and you can give this to me."

"Don't you want to know the reason for the gift?" asked the Medicine Man.

"I would have before but not now," the Warrior said, still looking into the darkness.

"Why not now? What has changed?"

"Many things have changed. Know that your gift is something that I do enjoy very much, but once it is gone, I miss it long after. So my enjoyment turns to a want that was not there before. If I will only have it for a moment, then unless that moment is forever, I don't want it."

"I understand what you are saying, but it's those moments in our life that we all will remember on our last day," he tried to explain to the boy.

"If I can forget this life and every day of it, then the fruit and the honey both will be forgotten also. There is only one thing that I would want to be remembered, and it is not by me but by all. This is the very thing I am asking you for now."

"What is it that you want?" asked the Medicine man.

"Someday soon I may leave this life, and this is something that I accept. Fear left me long ago. If I do leave here, then I welcome the next. For the ones that I leave behind, if ever they should want to remember me and tell others who are not here now of me, I would want them to have a name to say. My name. That way, others will know who I am always."

"You want a name?"

The boy had never mentioned this before. He had never

said that he was concerned with what he was called. How could he not have ever thought to consider this? It was something so basic yet so important. It was how every person in the simplest way was known to others. A name. He wanted a name, and why wouldn't he? He wasn't a tool to be used then put up until the next time he was needed, like an old pot or an ax. The boy was a person, just like the rest of the people. If only that were true. As much as the Medicine Man wished that it were, it was too late for this. The boy was far from anything the people were. In fact, in every way, he was nothing like the rest of the people.

"Yes, I do," he said.

"And what name would you have?" asked the Medicine Man.

"I am not sure, but I want one," the boy answered.

"Let us sleep, and in the morning, maybe we will have your name."

The boy could not wait for the day to come so that he would have his new name.

"Turtle? Tomorrow, I will have my own name," he said using his hands in the darkness of his hut. He could not wait for turtle to see it on him so that he could be known by the others. The boy believed that with his new name, like the rest, he would be accepted, and his loneliness would stop.

"I am…" he said as he practiced introducing himself so that he would be ready.

"I still need to tell you something that you need to know. Soon you will be asked to do something that you have been training for your whole life. You will use what you have learned from the black scrolls, and that is the reason for the gift." As the Medicine Man said this, the Warrior remained unmoving, staring off into the darkness.

"Leave me now. I will be ready when I am needed." The boy said, still looking out into the darkness.

CHAPTER 5

The Commander's men were on the tribe's side of the river, and there were enough of them that they had no worry of the pack, so the Medicine Man felt as many had already felt, cold—not only cold but bleak—and in that moment, all eyes fell on the Warrior, the one they had been forbidden to ever look at, even as he had grown up in their midst. He was one of the people, but unlike the rest, he had never known them, never had the love of his own mother, felt warmth in his grandmother's words. He had been denied a chance to play with the children as he grew. He had wished many times to be invited to swim just once, as well as do all the many other wonderful things that he had witnessed from in the center of them all.

He had never known what it felt like to be smiled at or even touched with care, not even looked at, but now he was their only hope. The people had no doubt that when asked, he would give up his life to save theirs. Tears filled their eyes as one by one they all looked at him for the very first time. At that moment they all saw him, and they would have given anything to take back what they had done. They could see that under his armor was one of the people, and a cry came up from them all that sent chills down the spines of the army that would be meeting him in battle on the next morning. He was one of the people, but first he was *Warrior*. His eyes could see their tears fall, but he could not hear their cries. This was good because all who did were weakened by it. Only he remained as he was, for the Medicine Man had done a good job preparing the Warrior. For this, he too wept with his people.

Although the Warrior was skilled in the deadly arts, he had never killed a man. In fact, he had never killed anything. Now on the eve of battle in which the Warrior was expected to stand against an army for the fate of his people. It was not likely the results would end well for the tribe. He was one, and they were many. Not only this, but these men were battle hardened. Now it was nearly time. As the Medicine Man sat, he thought of the things he had both seen and heard the day he and Teeosh had taken Drone to his father on the other side of the river. Even though it seemed as if the woman had been killed by Drone so long ago, the Medicine Man felt an uneasiness in his spirit. Both Teeosh and he had seen the way Drone had looked at them as they left him in the company of his father and the men of violence. Most of all, they could remember the words he had said.

"Remember, old man; remember this day, for it will be a day that all of your people will regret. You have seen my father's army, and soon you will feel it."

It was true he had seen the army of Drone's father. It was a vast army that stretched the length of the beach where they had been camped while they did repairs to their warships. They were docked in a small harbor, and the men had been laughing and joking when they had seen Drone and the others walk up and into the camp.

Instantly their full attention was on the new visitors who were walking through. Some of the men recognized Teeosh and Drone, but it was the Medicine Man that had their attention. This would be the first time that the two brothers would meet, and the Medicine Man had wished it were the last.

"Commander, your half-breed son has returned, along with his mother. The one that is called the Medicine Man also travels with them," a soldier reported.

"Are you sure that it is the Medicine Man?" asked the Commander. His eyes could not hide the hatred that had taken the whole of his life to create for his half-brother.

"Send them in," ordered the Commander as he sat up straight in his chair.

The soldier did as he was told, and in the next moment, the three were standing before him. The two brothers could not look away, their stares set on each other. The Medicine Man bowed his head, but the Commander remained still.

"I see you have returned my son. Who is this that stands with your mother?"

The Medicine Man had stepped forward to introduce himself when the Commander gave a nod to his guard. The guard drew back his long spear and attempted to shove the handle into the Medicine Man's back and knock him to the ground. He did not account for the Medicine Man's readiness, and instead, the guard was thrown down. Before he could move another step, he found the ends of ten spears in his face.

"Very well my half-brother. It seems that you can see behind you but not at all around you,"

"I don't need to see around myself to see the hate that you

have for me all over your face," said the Medicine Man as the spears were still being held to him.

"Why the visit after all this time? Was it to say, 'Hello, I'm your brother. Our father loved me more even though he didn't even know me'?" His hate for his brother could be heard in his voice.

"It was to bring your son home to you," said Teeosh.

"My son. That among all things would bring the most joy to my heart. My half-breed son is here to remind me of a moment of weakness forever. Very well then, leave the boy, and be gone before I turn the dogs loose," said the Commander. "One more thing before you leave—never come here again. When I am ready to see you, you will know it. Is that understood?"

"Yes," the two of them answered.

"I will come someday; I promise you."

With those words the two began the long journey home.

The ones with eyes of the sky were many. They were men of iron and violence. They were large and powerful soldiers. They did not ask of others; they took by force, for that was their way. The Medicine Man knew that it was only a matter of time before he would hear the soldiers war machines on their way to the village and his people. It was in this time that the Medicine Man set out on a journey to make a plea to the other tribes. He had told them of this new danger that they would all face someday. He had told them of the soldiers and of their thirst for both blood and power. He had said that his people had prepared a warrior and told of his purpose, which was to fight in war for what he and all of them believed in. Peace had always been their way. The people of the other tribes had all said this, but it was not the way of all men. This was what he tried to explain to the others, even though it was extremely hard for them to understand. So when the Medicine Man asked that they set aside their very best to help with the protection for the combined peoples on their side of the river, he did not know if they received his words, or if they fell away when he was gone. He could only hope that they would understand, and with his hope, he left.

■ ■ ■

The army of Drone's father moved at a steady pace through the high mountain passes and into the valley below. A scout appeared out of nowhere to report a large wolf pack just ahead.

"You hear that, boys? New pelts for the ones who think they can take them, the ones who have the courage to. Those of you who make the mistake of turning your backs to these pups might find in that choice the cost of your very life. Dire wolves are savage beasts that can carry a man away. You'll be taken into the dark and never seen again unless it's in a pile. I am sure they would rather put you in their bellies and make a quick meal of you instead. Dire wolf or not?" the Commander asked his men.

"*Wolf!*" the men yelled.

"Bring me a lamb, and I'll get the trap set," said the Commander, who wore the pelt of the largest wolf that any had ever seen. He had taken his trophy in his youth when he was on his way to immortality.

The lamb was brought, and as the scent of fresh blood was

released into the air, the wolves soon stopped their own march and redirected their full attention to what would soon be their next meal. They moved swiftly through the forest toward where the men had prepared the trap. The scent of the lamb's blood was heavy in the pack's noses but not enough for them to overlook the unmistakable scent of their favorite meal, men! The wolves, also knowing that men were sometimes extremely dangerous, approached very carefully.

"Quiet!" ordered the Commander. "They're close! Hold steady, and loose on my command." The early evening sky shone with vivid reds and deep blues. The air was cool, and the men all held their breath as a pair of yellow eyes appeared at the edge of the tree line. It was soon accompanied by many more sets until the woods seemed to be alive.

Sweat began to drop from the soldiers' brows as the wolves all held their position in the trees.

"What are they waiting for?" said a soldier who was eager for a fight. The men were prepared to let loose their arrows when a large dire came from out of the woods behind them, grabbing a man. The wolf was gone, back to where he had come and out of sight. Two more wolves followed close behind the first, both grabbing a soldier each. The commotion of the men being pulled down and dragged into the forest had the other men breaking their line as they turned their heads in order to see the forest behind them.

"Behind you!" the Commander yelled.

With that the men took up a defensive position to their rear. Their armor was heavy, and they moved clumsily on the trail. The air was cold, but these men dripped with sweat. The wolves' fur kept them one with the shadows as they evaporated into thin air, then returned in an instant like smoke rising from the charred coals of a forest fire. They seemed to be there, then not. This was the way of the wolves, princes of the forest who would not surrender these lands without first being remembered.

As soon as the men turned to defend their rear, the wolves in the tree line advanced, running past the wounded lamb and straight for the exposed backs of the unsuspecting soldiers. Screams were heard as the wolves took many more men, before the men on horseback and with long spears joined the fight. The reach of the men was more than the wolves could overcome, and one by one they were all run through by the men on horseback. There was not even one that would escape.

Besides the men, many horses had become spooked at the sight of the wolves, leaping to their deaths after they had scaled the fence rails of a makeshift corral. Several dozen fully grown wolves in all were run through by the men on horseback. The soldiers' spirits were raised even higher at the expense of the wolves' future, and many men would be all dressed up in their new wolf hides for the next day's work.

"If tomorrow goes as well as tonight, we'll continue our advance into the land. I'm sure with a little determination we will be able to find others, and run through the lot of them. Then finally we can be done with the tribes," said Drone, eager to show the people their mistake in returning him to his father.

"That is what I intend to do son," said the Commander. He had planned for this day for many years. Knowing that this time was finally upon him, as well as his son's eagerness to help, made him proud.

"Then it's settled. We will have no need to concern ourselves with these people ever again," Drone continued as he planned in his mind the many ways he would make the people pay.

"We could keep the strongest women and children. Put them all to the fields so that an outpost could be built. A place for future men and beasts to await orders of advancement into the land."

"Ambition is a quality I admire son," said the Commander, pleased with Drone's eagerness.

Drone could only imagine the Medicine Man's face just before he cut it from his skull.

■ ■ ■

The army of Drone's father was what the people were not, an instrument of death in the flesh, and the Warrior was just one man. The soldiers were trained to use weapons of steel, as well as war machines. How would he be able to find inside himself what it would take to overcome and save the people? That was the easy part. The Warrior loved only one thing in this life, and that was his only friend, Turtle.

It saddened the Medicine Man that his job of preparing the Warrior was something that required pain, and now it was nearly time to unleash that pain in the boy. Even though it could very well save the people, it was to be more pain for the Warrior, more than he had ever felt before. A feeling of sorrow came over the Medicine Man, and had it not been for the sake of the entire tribe, he did not know that he would be able to do what he must. He knew that it was the tribe's only hope and that it had to be done. He had done this for his people, but at that moment he wished he had not. The people were changed by what they had all seen that day during battle, in the midst of rage directed at another. The people were not the same, and this was the beginning of reality—the day they lost Eden.

This time was known as the "Wandering," and it was the hope of the people to return to Eden and the ways of their ancestors. They were not made to exist in this reality. The longer they did, the further from Eden they fell.

This was the price that the people paid for war, so the first war cry was heard, and it was for a small turtle—small but very, very much loved.

This is why the people had called it a war cry, because as he cried, he released his inner power, destroying everything he saw. What he saw was Drone's father's army.

As the Warrior's mother Sutkey welcomed the Medicine Man into her home, a look of concern took shape on her face.

"Why do you look so down?" she asked.

"Tonight, is a night like no other," he replied.

"Yes, it is. He will be fine. You have prepared him in the greatest of skill and discipline. He is who we cannot be," she said.

"Yes, I believe this, but he is also who we are, a mere shadow, but yes this is true. When I look at him, I know that he is this way because of me. I did this to your son," said the Medicine Man.

"No. Murder did this to my son. War is doing the very thing that he has become. Know that he is no longer just my son, but he is also the son of us all. What he shall do tomorrow is more than any one person can ever be responsible for. We are the people; he is our son. Tomorrow he will prove why he was necessary, so that our hearts can begin to heal. He will remind us all why war has no place with the people. Not only ours but all in this world that we call home. Those who will lie down tomorrow for the last time are all our sons."

"But if he dies, I don't believe I will be able to bare it. The life he was denied is something that every one of the people have enjoyed. He was never given that choice, and now he is here with only this night to hold on to. He is alone, and this is where he has been his whole life, alone. If he doesn't win, then he will have been here without ever really living," said the Medicine Man.

"Then he will just have to win," Sutkey said with all the hope of every one of the people in her words.

"Is there anything else you want to say?" She could see that there was more on his mind.

"Your son wishes to have a name. I could think of no one else but his mother to give it to him," the Medicine Man said, hoping she could help the boy with a name all his own.

"A name? His name would be the same as yours. That's what I would have called him before tonight," said Sutkey as her eyes looked to the ground.

"You are the only father he has ever known," she answered.

The Medicine Man had never considered this and he wondered why he had not. "Well, that is what I would have called him." She set her gaze back to the fire as she continued. "Now that this night is upon us and we sit on the eve of a new day, one that we are not prepared to know, it doesn't seem to suit him. So I'm sorry, but I don't have a name for him."

CHAPTER 6

It was the next morning. The sky was gray, and the air was cold. The boy had been waiting on the name that would be his. He could feel the vibration of the Medicine Man's footsteps on the ground beneath his feet. As the door to the hut opened, they came face-to-face. The Medicine Man knew that the days of thinking of him as a boy were nearly over. Standing just inside the door, the Warrior began to speak in the way he knew.

"Look at me! I have wanted this for so long, but now I realize that my name has already been chosen by the Creator. This is the name that I will be remembered by, Warrior."

The Medicine Man knew this was true. The Warrior was told of his reason for being. He thought for a brief moment before understanding that he could not change what had been done, causing him to believe that it must be his destiny, so he was not afraid.

He was told that on the next day he would be shown the men who had done this terrible thing that was meant to destroy him, and in the Warrior's thinking, it almost had.

"The men are of steel and armor; it is these men who came as you slept, and killed Turtle. These men shall return to hear your answer, which is when you may return what is owed," said the Medicine Man as he pulled out from behind his back

Turtles lifeless body. The Warrior's eyes opened wide as he took Turtle into his hands, falling to his knees. Tears had begun to fall from his face.

"What is owed? How can I ever return what is owed? You say they will come to hear my answer. I have no answer any man could ever understand. The ones who will receive my answer are all ghosts. They will have this night, but when I take them from this life, they will know that what they did to Turtle is the reason. On that day, they will see the sun rise for the last time."

Hearing this, the Medicine Man knew he had done all he could to prepare the boy.

"Leave me," he said. "I want to be alone."

"Is there anything I can do for you?" asked the Medicine Man.

"Only if you can make it so that I was never born. If you cannot do this, then no," replied the Warrior. "What do words matter now? Turtle is gone, so I truly am alone, something that I always thought I knew. Now I know what it really is to be alone and it is far worse than anything I have ever felt before."

With these words, the Medicine Man could see that the boy was gone; all that remained was the Warrior. He would not sleep that night, with just the memory of his only friend Turtle in his now broken heart.

As his tears continued to fall, the sun could not come fast enough. It was to be the first but not the last time the people would witness battle. It would be something that would change their lives for the rest of their days.

The village was quiet, and the smell of the fires coming

from the people's homes was everywhere. It seemed to be a normal night in the village, but there were none of the sounds that were usually heard on any other night—no men talking, women cooking, or children playing with one another. If not for the fires, you would not have known that this village had people who called it home.

Slowly, one by one, the people all started walking from their homes toward the center of the village. None spoke as they gathered near the Warrior's hut.

A man appeared carrying an armful of wood, and he began to make a fire as others also brought wood. Soon the whole village had gathered there, and still no one spoke. Their somber mood could be seen on their faces as they all stood in the light of the fire. All the people knew that this could be their last night, and they wanted to spend it together, with the ones they loved. They were the people, the ones who made this place home.

The Medicine Man looked over them all as he thought of the moment he had let them first see the boy who was now a man. He had slowly walked across the space where the people had gathered, toward the hut of the Warrior. He could feel the eyes of all the people on him. The sounds of the night seemed to come out of the forest, and to the ears of the people. It was as if they carried an urgent message. The frogs joined crickets, along with the occasional owl, to perform a beautiful symphony, as if the Creator himself had composed a song for the moment the people would first see him. The one that would hold their lives in his hands. As he approached the door that had been bleached by the sun, it glowed bright under the full moon, along with the moss that had grown on the north side of the hut, which was now covered with a light frost.

The rest of the stones that held the boy from all life were dark and cold without a fire to warm them. Without a sound to let the people know that he was there just on the other side of that door. Alone, he waited for the moment that he would be seen.

The Medicine Man slowly reached for the door but suddenly stopped, pulling his hand back to his side. How would he explain to them all about the man that they would see when that door opened.

What the people would witness was something that they knew nothing of. As he turned back to the people, he could see that their stares were set on him. Then without warning the creak of the door could be heard as it slowly opened on its own and out of the darkness came the Warrior. It was the first time that the people would see the one that they had always known was there. The people could all see that what they had feared was real. It was real, and he was proof of it. War was coming, and when it came, it meant to kill them.

His face did not have the lines made from a smile, so that he didn't seem real, his skin pale under the turtle-shell armor, without the effects of the sun to show his age. A mask had been cut from the turtle shells, and he put the mask to his face so only the cold stare of his eyes could be seen. They were like the ice that formed on the river during the coldest winters, so hard that even stone hammers could not easily break it. Clear enough to look into, but at the same time a man could see his own reflection in it. His eyes held no lies, open for all to see.

He was a man of stone, and still he walked, and the people could not look away.

What had changed the boy into what stood before them all? Behind those stone walls, he had changed, and the army that marched to the village at that very moment did not have the grip on the people it had just a short time before. If those men were monsters, then the Warrior was what monsters feared.

The people knew that he was the one that held their lives in his hands. They realized that they didn't even know his name. He was ready to give up his life to save theirs, and they all just wanted to shout out his name.

"Look Mama, I can see the Warrior," a boy said.

Suddenly the people all began to shout out, "Warrior! Warrior! Warrior!

They all wanted him to know that they had saw him and that he was needed. The Warrior's stare seemed to look into the people, and the calls of his name suddenly stopped.

The Warrior could see the people all holding their breath as they just stared. He became aware that he was holding his breath as well. He waited a moment more, then exhaled. The people also releasing their own, many becoming aware of the spell they all seemed to be under. They could not believe what the boy had become, with his not knowing of things like caring, family, or consideration. These were all strangers and simply were not known, along with home, friendship, and the greatest of all, love.

None of these were known by him, and the people wondered if he even knew they existed. If he did know, they seemed not to be missed. Maybe there was something in his cold eyes that said he might have an idea that he was not complete. He seemed to know that he was without a part that the others had. A part that could let him understand why they all just stared at him as if he were something that they had never seen and could never understand. He felt their disbelief in his existence, and they could not look away. The moment felt like it was as much a dream as it was real. A man started to say something, having felt an urge to be heard, but he could only fumble over a word or two before the eyes of the Warrior met his. The man seemed to melt back into himself and his silence joined the rest of the people. His movement was direct as he walked, his path unchanging by anything or anyone. As he came closer to the people, they began to part before him so that he could pass through them all.

The Warrior looked back to the Medicine Man and began to speak in the way that was understood by him.

"Tell them what I say, leave nothing out. Make sure they all understand what it is I say. Know that after I am done, they may return to the comfort of not knowing what it is I am."

"OK," said the Medicine Man as he tried to clear his throat.

"Tell them, even if they do not understand what I have become, it does not matter. I am not for them to understand. I have a purpose, and it is that purpose that I am here for. Tell them to release themselves from the fear of the things that have a hold on them, so they will see that I am not afraid. They will never understand why, but they should know that it is not for them to know why. Only know that I am Warrior, and I will know it for them."

The Warriors face did not move or show any sign of

knowing or understanding what it was they were trying to express to him as they called out his name.

He found his way through the darkness, and a light to show the way was absent as the shadows held to him as if he were their home. Still the people could not look away. They struggled for a clear look at the boy whom they all knew as the Warrior. The more they tried to see him, the less he seemed to show. A blur of coldness surrounded him, and he, in the next moment, faded away into the night and was gone.

"How long until they are here?" asked the Warrior.

"Soon, by the next morning, I am sure of it," replied the Medicine Man.

"What are these ones doing to prepare?" asked the Warrior as he motioned back toward where the people were.

"Why do they not prepare," asked the boy.

"They have done all they can do. These people do not know the ways of violence; it is something they do not understand. Their only hope is in you. If you knew the things that they know, you would see that they are like children in the midst of wolves. They do not know anything but hope when it comes to these things. Don't you see how their eyes are as big as the moon; seeing you is like seeing the sun for the first time as a man—it does not have to be the end for these people, but it will be if you do not win."

"How can I say that I won? Even if I send these men into the bleak, I will still have lost without Turtle."

"This is true, but you will still have the life that the Creator gave you so that you could have known Turtle."

"What is so good about living a life that is full of loss and loneliness?" asked the warrior.

"Knowing that one day you could have something to call your own, just like before. Their lives are in your hands. They do not know the teachings of the Black Scrolls. These things they will never know, or risk losing who they are. Who the people have always been, as well as our home. It is you who will know this for them" replied the medicine man.

"What about me?" the boy asked.

"I'm sorry, but you will always have one foot in the people's home and one in a place covered in the blood of the ones that you will be sending into the next."

"Then I will hold their hands so that they will not lose their way. I will be with them when they meet whatever awaits them on the other side. I know that my time is short here. So, I hope that I am remembered even if I will never really be known."

So, it was the eve before battle, and it was as if all time stood still, holding its breath for that moment.

CHAPTER 7

As the army traveled the last part of the pass, they began to reach the flat ground. As they did, the Commander received word.

"Commander, the men in the front have reached the village," reported one of his higher-ranking men. His manner was that of a soldier. His eyes forward, he sat straight up on his horse, waiting for the Commander's orders.

The Commander stopped, remaining still as he took in a deep breath of the crisp morning air, holding it for another moment before slowly releasing it back out.

"Do you smell that?" he asked of his second in command. "That is the smell of victory…all we do now is take it."

"Of course Commander, victory is certain."

Both of these men had been sitting high on their horses, their polished armor shined bright in the early morning sun.

Their horses' armor clinked with every step, causing an eerie silence to fall over the surrounding forest. The soldiers felt the chill of that silence rush through them as they remembered the cries of the people that had come to haunt them the night before as they traveled the high pass.

Then from out of that silence came a single call of a raven

as it sat atop a tall tree. Suddenly that call was answered by another raven and then another.

The treetops began to sway, as ravens along with crows, began to gather in their branches. They seemed to be shouting all at once as a sudden stream of vultures came flying high above the Commander's army. They gathered as they rode the updraft higher and higher, flying in large circles. Their long necks allowed them to hang their heads as they soared, looking down to the ground far below. They filled the sky as they seemed to come from every direction. A dark storm circled the army, making no sound as it soared high above, blocking the sun so that the army marched in its shadow.

The soldiers' horses began to step nervously as they became difficult to control. The men struggling to hold their formation as some of the animals started to rear up and the armies lines were sent forward in uneven rows.

The screams of the dark spectators that lined the trees branches made it impossible for the soldiers' commands to be heard by the men.

"What's going on? Have you ever seen anything like this?" one of the soldiers asked the man marching beside him.

"No, never, and I've seen more battles than I can count." The unfamiliar audience caused him to shake his body back and forth, trying to rid himself of it all. His hands became slick as sweat began to drench them.

All the men's eyes were opened wide as they turned their heads to view the dark swarms that filled the sky. The people watched as the soldiers entered a clear space that was outlined with the trees that were part of the dense forest. This had served as the tribes ceremonial area.

It started at dawn on the morning after the extermination of the pack the night before. Many of the men were tired barely having their wits about them. It did not matter—the work of the day would be light. The "bush babies," as the soldiers called the people, had no army.

"Sticks and stones!" they said, laughing as they were just reaching the position where they expected to find the Warrior and his people. As they did, they took up their weapons and adjusted them into the ready position, every man feeling the slaughter would be soon. Then it was time.

Drone rode up front, next to his father, to show the way.

"So you say the bush babies have conjured up some type of Warrior?" the Commander asked Drone as they approached the village.

"Something like that Father, but he will see his own blood by the edge of my sword today," Drone said; his eagerness to make the people suffer could be seen on his face.

"I will be proud to witness it," said the Commander as the two rode on in anticipation of Drone's victory.

As the army moved forward, the ground shook with the combined force of so many horses and boots beating down in unison. The men knowing that in a short time, these lands would all be the Commanders. The soldiers eager to show their skills in battle so that they could be rewarded with lands and titles of their own. Many of the men playing out in their heads the brutality that they would show during the fight in order to stand out from the rest.

The anticipation of blood causing some of the men's mouths to water, knowing that they were close. Many of the men noticing how beautiful the tribe's home was, causing them to think of the shame it would be to disturb this place with the terrors of war. It was free of these ghosts now, and that would all be over soon.

As the army began to round the final bend, expecting to see the village; but instead what they saw was the Medicine Man leading another man out on to the field. As he did the Commander could see that the man wore an armor of turtle shells. This was something that he had never seen before, causing a smile to appear on the commanders face.

Surely this was not meant to be the answer the people had prepared for him. An old man directing the other as if he were the conductor of great and important things.

"What is this?" asked the Commander as he took in the scene.

"That's him father, the Warrior," Drone said as he sat atop his horse, his eyes fixed on the Medicine Man.

"He's barely a man, almost a boy, is what he looks like to me," said the Commander as he tried to take in what he was looking at.

"My brother must be crazy," the Commander said aloud as he shook his head while taking hold of his helmet and putting it on. He pressed it down snug so that it would not move, blocking his view as he swung his sword during the battle. Next, his chain-mail-covered gloves were pulled tight to his hands so that his grip on his sword was firm.

"This is a home fit for the king," he said, and he could see himself atop a new throne, one he would make himself.

Laughter swept across the ranks as the army began to clear the bend and file into the space where the village had been. Looking across the field, the soldiers were surprised by what they saw.

"Do these people want to die?" one of the men said, shaking his head.

"They must, if this is the only way they are attempting to oppose us," the man continued; wiping sweat from his forehead.

"Why didn't anyone tell me it would be turtle soup today?" said one of the men as he laughed with the rest.

As they laughed, they noticed that just off on the closest ridge in the midst of the trees stood the whole of the tribe, there to witness the events that were sure to come, and with those events, the fate of the people. The last of the soldiers filed in and took their place on what would now be the battlefield.

The Commander's sword-hand suddenly rose, causing a silence to fall over his men. These would be the people's last moments before the sickness and its effects would take them away from the days before.

As they peered across the meadow, Drone asked his father a question, "Sword or ax?"

"Surprise me son, but don't make it too quick. Make him squirm, then scream, and finally let the men hear him beg," replied the Commander.

"Anything else?" Drone said as he stood up on the back of his horse. His eyes were fixed on the field in front of him.

"How about putting the head of my brother atop the staff he carries?" replied the Commander.

"Consider it done," Drone said, more than pleased with his father's request.

At that moment the two men exchanged looks.

"Well, what are you waiting for?" asked the Commander, pushing his head toward the open field.

With that, Drone charged the field alone, prepared to do just as his father had asked. Drone was at a full run when the Medicine Man uttered a single word, unleashing a storm of destruction…

"*Them!*" said the Medicine Man as he pointed his finger at the army of Drones father.

■ ■ ■

Drone had seen the mouth of the old man move as if to say a single word; with that, the head of the man on the field rose up. Drone noticed that tears dropped from the Warrior's face, giving Drone even more confidence, causing him to push his horse even harder. Drone noticed that in the Warrior's hands was something covered in blood. As he got just within range of his ball and chain and thought how clever he was to surprise his father with his choice of weapon, he saw that the object was a small turtle. He began to think a thought at that moment, but he never finished it. He never finished it because he was dead.

The Warrior's spear slammed through the front of Drone's skull, then continued across the meadow, impaling another soldier through his armor. The mouths of the entire army dropped open. The men could not believe what they had seen.

They looked from the field to the Commander, but he seemed to be in a sort of daze. He was without any type of reaction as he just stared forward at the motionless body of Drone on the field.

He had only a moment to contemplate the fact that he had just seen the life of his son extinguished in an instant before he too found his own life in jeopardy. The Warrior was among his ranks, stabbing and slashing the men at will. Dead soldiers bodies left in his wake as he quickly moved through the army like the blade of a sharpened ax through seasoned wood. The sound of bones being crushed behind useless armor combined with the sounds of flesh tearing open, releasing the screams of the men who received his touch. The screams filled the sky, and they themselves were the dinner bell that the ravens and buzzards of all known existence were waiting on.

The sky became dark with the swarms of the hungry from above, and the blood had only begun to flow. Man after man was torn down where he stood. Feeble attempts to defend themselves were met with swift death. Decapitated men's bodies were left still standing. They held weapons tightly in the ready position, but without a head to give them direction, the bodies quickly fell to the earth to accompany their heads. Soon panic started to set in as the men waved their swords back and forth, swinging at an enemy they could not see. A blur of death was among them, and they were powerless to stop it.

The Commander, in an attempt to save his own life, began to shout orders to the few remaining men who were strong enough to keep their sanity amid complete terror.

"Shield wall on me!" the Commander screamed, prompting his men back into their fighting position. They quickly formed a wall of iron and steel in hopes of defending themselves from the advance of the Warrior.

"Long spears, hold fast!" the Commander shouted out to his spear men, causing them to instantly position themselves for the death blows they would offer. Their legs were shaking so much and there were so many of them that a chatter rose to meet the darkness that flew just above their heads. Tears could be seen in the eyes of several of the soldiers, and they could not hold back their cries, showing all that they had lost the fight inside themselves. Other soldiers quickly pulled them to the ground killing them where they lay.

"I don't want to die," a soldier yelled, and after that die is exactly what he did.

On the Warrior's approach, as he was just in range of the long spears, he turned to his side, just missing the blades as they were thrust at him. He was quickly past them and at the base of the shield wall. Finding the soldier whose fear had overtaken him ever so slightly so that he retreated just for an instant, and the Warrior had found his hole. He quickly slipped through the small space, causing panic to take hold of every man. The long spears began stabbing eagerly at any movement in front of them. These men were hoping to save their own lives and end the Warrior's. Instead all they found were the backs of their own men as they were violently stabbed one after another until the wall was gone, replaced by a mountain of men who died at the hands of their own fellow soldiers. These men had forgotten all they had been trained to do for fear of the Warrior.

Then it was their turn. Many dropped their weapons in retreat. The ones who tried to fight were killed first. Others, seeing the hopelessness in either path, turned their own blades on themselves so that they would not feel the Warrior's. They could be heard mumbling to themselves as the moment of their unexpected decision came closer and closer with every step that the Warrior took toward them.

There had indeed been a slaughter on that day, just as the soldiers had expected, only it was their own. The Commander, being one of the few who was still on horseback, chose to flee, and in the heat of battle, he escaped.

That was the one mistake that the Warrior had made on that terrible day. It was his only mistake; the rest were made by what were the men of violence. They had dealt their own hand and in that hand they lost everything. So it was the day the first war cries were heard by the people, and they were for a small turtle. Small but very, very much loved.

When the battle was over, not a single soldier was left standing. The ones who still lived squirmed in pain all over the battlefield. A total of six men were added to the tribe, nursed to health by the people. Two of them eventually left so that they could return to their families. Four of them chose to remain there with the people, eventually finding wives and extending the tribe by many more.

The birds, along with the worms, it would seem, were the true victors of all. The people were called back to the village and left to pick up and dispose of the carnage. There was no need to leave now since the wolves would not be there to claim their winter home, and the Warrior stood silently in the shadows, holding his dear lost friend in his hands. Without Turtle, he would spend the better part of his day and night alone. The battle was over, and that was the result of love turned to rage, then to a longing, and finally a numbness. A spectator to his own reality, a lonely one without another, and he wished it were him being lowered into the ground. At least the worms would be there. At least he would know that somebody or something else could see him. He felt like something that did not have a word or a way, but it was how he felt.

■ ■ ■

"How did he feel?" Benjamin asked the old one.

The story had everyone on the edge of their seat.

"Back then there was no word to describe it, but today we call it invisible. He was just alone. Without anyone to see his pain, he felt that he did not have a place. He just didn't know what that was called because no one had ever been where he was.

"There was a new reality, and that was where he had gone. It would always have a hold on him for the rest of his days. Another price paid for war," the old one answered, and he could see that everyone's eyes were opened wide as they hung on every word that came from his mouth.

■ ■ ■

The Medicine Man had lied to the boy, killing his only friend Turtle. He had done this to save the people, but in his heart he felt he was wrong.

As he looked at the Warrior, he could see that his pain was very real, and it was only just beginning. It seemed his whole life had been lived in pain, in one form or another. His purpose was fulfilled. What now? Realizing he had taken the whole life of the man in front of him, having nothing to offer in return. The Medicine Man just stared, his mind racing back through the years to the day the boy was born.

Suddenly a child walked up to the Warrior and said, "Thank you" as he hugged him.

It was his first hug, and it filled him with a new feeling. A feeling that was better than alone. One by one the rest of the tribe took their place in line to thank him, to hug him, to introduce themselves, and to properly welcome him home. Last of all stood the Warrior's mother. She had waited his whole life for this, and when it was finally happening she became overwhelmed with emotions. She held her son, and it seemed she would never let go. Finally she did, but it was him that held on. That was a day of homecoming, but it also was the beginning of rebirth, for as the ravens feasted, their lot was cast. She would be the greatest of all warriors, and she was not yet born.

CHAPTER 8

The Warrior never adjusted to being part of the tribe. It was suggested that the Warrior could hunt with the hunters. Despite having killed so many on that dreadful day, it was not something that he could do to an animal. Until his first battle, the Warrior had only known the company of animals. Animals like Turtle, as well as birds and field mice, along with foxes and many other forest creatures. So he spent most of his days alone.

"What's wrong?" the Medicine Man asked the Warrior. He could see that something was bothering him.

"It has been many seasons since I've came to be known by the rest.

I can't understand why have I not been given a smile from the others."

"I don't know that one can be given unless one has been given first." replied the Medicine Man.

"How can I give a smile when I have none to give?" asked the Warrior.

"You must first find a smile of your own" said the Medicine Man.

■ ■ ■

The Warrior took a wife, and after some time, she was with child. Life was returning to normal when word came from one of the hunters. He had been hunting far off in the high country, when the tracks of soldiers had been found. They were few, but they were there. Suddenly a stir came over the people, and once again, all eyes fell on the Warrior.

"What trouble could just a few soldiers cause? They have seen the Warrior in battle. Surely, they would not think to harm the people."

Even so, the Medicine Man had worry in his heart. It was true that they were few, but these were no ordinary soldiers. They were trained assassins, and in this they were unmatched.

Blood Disciples were a group of men renowned for assassination. These killers would stop at nothing to accomplish it, and their reason for being on the people's side of the river was the Warrior's head.

"How many days off were the tracks?" asked the Medicine Man.

"Two, maybe three days off. They also travel with beasts," said the hunter.

Hearing this, the Medicine Man knew exactly who they would be dealing with. Only one type of soldier traveled with the dire, the Blood Disciples. The Medicine Man's worry was confirmed and he would need to prepare.

"Why do you have worry on your face?" the hunter asked.

He received no answer. This new threat was not only very real to Warrior, but it was also one that the Medicine Man was familiar with.

For this reason, he would not speak to any other person

on the matter, except for the Warrior. The Medicine Man knew that he would need all the help he could get to overcome what he was about to face.

"I know that this should be a time of rest and family for you, but I have been told by one of the hunters that the tracks of soldiers have been found. They are heading to the village. I know of the men that are coming. They mean to kill you, and they will stop at nothing until this is done," said the Medicine Man.

"How do you know so much about these people?"

"Let me tell you a story about the people who call the land of rock and thorn home. These are the things that I came to know when I was still a young man. I learned these things in the times I spent there.

The other side of the river is barren, with only rocks and nothing in the way of nourishment as vegetation is scarce. Thorns cover the land, and it is extremely dangerous to travel on account of the many viper breeds that call that side of the river home. It is a dark and forbidding land. The ones who live there are men of war and violence. Far off in the distance looms the outline of the Thunder Mountains, home of the Boneface tribe, the only one of the ancient tribes that lived among the men of violence. These men had long golden hair and bushy beards, and their eyes were the color of a cloudless sky. Their mouths were full of rotten teeth, and their skin was as white as snow. They wore plate armor that showed their family crest of lions, eagles, or whatever beast they chose to represent their clans. All of them rode atop large warhorses that also wore plated armor used to protect them on the battlefield. They built large stone fortresses with tall towers that flew the flags of the warlords who ruled them. They were masters of the sea, commanding large warships that they often used to attack unsuspecting people from far-off lands. They took, burning and killing any who were unfortunate enough to be seen by these raiders of the sea.

"Very few of the people had ever set foot on that side of the river. Of the ones who had, I was the only one who had ever returned. My father was from the land of rock and thorn. When I first crossed to the other side of the river, I was not seen for a very long time by the people. Then one day after many years, I returned, but it seemed that my time away had changed me.

"In the time that I was gone, I had taken up with a group of killers known as the Blood Disciples, assassins of the highest degree.

"These men were a breed that I could not continue to be a part of, nor could I allow them to continue to corrupt men with their teachings. These writings are known as the Black Scrolls. They are powerful, and if the Blood Disciples were allowed to possess them any longer, I believe that they would have caused this age to end with all that was good being destroyed. The people's home possibly becoming like the other side of the river. That was something I could not let happen, so I took from their brotherhood these, their most sacred of writings.

"This land was no place for the people, and none should ever go there. It was full of robbery and the roads were littered with rubbish. Corpses hung from trees anywhere that a tree could be found. Public floggings and beheadings could be seen daily as the warlords were merciless when it came to upholding their rule. Children played alongside open trenches that ran down the roads causing a foul stench all around. The shelters that the common people lived in were covered in grime as soot from their oil lamps covered everything. It was the only way to light the narrow paths as they traveled. The sound of horses' hooves on cobblestones could be heard, as well as the mooing of cows or the congested breathing of pigs. They were pinned up alongside the small shelters everywhere. Stray dogs fought for the scraps of food that were thrown out the windows of the shelters and onto the roads. They could even be seen carrying the limbs from corpses that they would take from the trees all over. If not for the river, not even the vipers would have stayed there. These are the men that will be coming to retrieve your head."

■ ■ ■

The Commander had returned to the land of rock and thorn; he had sent word to the Blood Disciples that he was prepared to pay a king's ransom for the head of the Warrior, and as expected, they answered the call. The Commander had used these men before when he had a wealthy neighbor fall to an unfortunate demise at the hands of these killers. So, the Commander knew what to expect when dealing with them.

They boasted weapons of never before seen savagery, weapons of fire, and a mastery of savage beasts, which included dire wolves and Barak eagles, as well as venomous vipers. *All* these assassins were skilled with any weapon that they chose to put in their hand. Their leader was a medium-sized individual who spoke in a faint voice and was unwilling to make eye contact. His name was never given, nor was it asked. Despite this, all the disciples' attention was on him. As he spoke, his eyes seemed to be fixed in a gaze into nowhere.

"And the price will be double the last time, to be paid in full now." As fast as he spoke it, it was paid. These men lived by a creed, and death was the only penalty for breaking it. "I have received word that the Warrior has already laid your army to waste, as well as your son. They say you were barely able to escape with your life. Surely, you would pay more to save your own life than just to gain the wealth of a neighbor. I am sure the Warrior is bothered that you are able to still breathe."

"For the head of the Warrior, I am willing to pay not only well but very well," the Commander replied.

"Tell us about this man who lays armies to waste," said one of the disciples.

"How does one man accomplish this act?"

"Or was it a really badly trained army?" said another one of the disciples.

"I'll say," said a woman with the smile of an angel who also lived by the creed. "At least the Commander made it out. That's all that matters when it comes to filling my pockets," she said with that smile.

"Fill them he will," said another one of the disciples, all laughing openly in the presence of the Commander. These words cut deep into the Commander. He had not had a moment's rest since he had witnessed Drone and his men cut down by the Warrior.

"Yes, this is all true, he did lay my army to waste, as well as my son. I was lucky to escape with my own life. Your pockets will be more than full if you indeed can bring me his head," he continued, his hands trembling slightly as he recalled the events of that day.

"But what is not true is that my army was poorly trained; my men were the finest group of soldiers ever seen, disciplined beyond comparison, many men having fallen to them without any hope. Because of them, my land and gold have increased to all that you see, enough to fill your pockets ten times more. This is the army you speak of. These men scaled the walls at Rausm, the type that caused the siren kings to jump from the towers of Baronmos—these men burned Harish to the ground, and not one stone remained on another. Rivers of blood flowed as the masses reached the sky with the dead. Your children have seen joyful days and peaceful nights with no worry of dires, and the proof they wore on their backs, having never seen defeat until that day.

"You see, what happened to my men at the hands of this Warrior is what cannot be explained. The man whose head you claim to be able to retrieve is not a man.

"Do men move as a blur? Do they leave battle-hardened soldiers without their nerve, as if children in the midst of a dragon, insanity taking hold of their mind during battle? My men turned their own swords on themselves, not willing to accept this Warrior's blade."

The disciples could see that the Commander did not blink

his eyes as he spoke. They seemed to be unwilling to allow him to concentrate on anything but his surroundings. His hands trembled as he tried to hide them behind his back. "What you are being asked is no easy task. Surely many if not all of you will be cut down before your payment is spent, and those who do survive will know that only the grace of God can be said to be the reason. So laugh but enjoy it, for it may be the last time your heads are attached to do so," said the Commander. "Now I hope that this has answered your question. Is there anything else?"

"There is one more matter that is of the utmost importance to us," replied one of the disciples.

"Yes, what is it?"

"It is the matter of the Black Scrolls, the writings that were taken from our house by the one they call the Medicine Man," the disciple said.

"These writings I do not know of, but what concern are they to me?" the Commander asked, uneasy with the topic.

"None really, only that upon the delivery of the Warrior's head, we shall collect these writings and return them to our land," the one with no name said.

"That is no concern of mine. All I need is the head," the Commander replied, hoping that it would satisfy them and they would be gone.

"We go to retrieve what you have paid for," said the disciple.

■ ■ ■

"What do you make of his story?" asked one of the assassins of their leader.

"I make nothing of it. I look past it as if it is already done. I have already consumed him and taken his power, and what is left of him is in a pile that I left in the woods along with a meal of potted meat and onions. That is what I think of it," replied their leader.

CHAPTER 9

"Warrior!" a voice rang out over the whole of the people's paradise, which was their home. "Warrior!" Once again the voice boomed. "Come to receive your enlightenment by way of the boys." When he said boys, he meant sixteen full-grown dire wolves.

With a nod of the assassin's head, the wolves were off without a sound, quickly covering ground as they moved across the forest floor, and it seemed that nothing would slip by them.

The largest of the wolves, a black male, took the lead position and set the pace for the rest. He quickly was able to find the Warrior's scent. The disciples had been able to retrieve an arrow earlier that morning from the place that had been set aside for the Warrior to train. The Dires quickly came upon a grove of brush that the large male was sure the Warrior was hiding in, and as he and two other large wolves darted in to collect their prize; they were quickly replaced by more wolves prepared to do the same.

Within minutes all that remained at the edge of the thicket were two female wolves, who were being pushed by their handler to join their pack in the brush. They both were unwilling and snapped violently. Not hearing any noise or commotion coming from inside the hiding place, along with the females' refusal to enter, told the handler that his fate had already been sealed. As he turned to run, he came face-to-face with a large black male wolf that seemed to be set on making a meal of him. As the wolf took the head of the disciple in his mouth, crushing it with no effort, the two female wolves grabbed ahold of his legs, ripping them from his body in a violent tug-of-war. The remaining thirteen wolves made easy work of the hooded eagles who were blind to their fate, as well as their handler, the snake charmer, and the girl with a smile that was all but beautiful on that morning.

Once they had finished, they all gathered at the feet of the Warrior, one by one licking his face in a show of appreciation to him before disappearing into the brush. Their howls could be heard for many more nights until one day they stopped, hopefully to someday be heard again. Like that the disciples' numbers were cut in half.

The remaining disciples regrouped, preparing a hole dug deep enough for what would happen next.

"Since he loves his people so much, let's see how he likes watching them burn," said one of the disciples. With that, they produced clay pots covered in pitch and filled with oil. A small fuse came up and out of the top. They lit the pots and quickly threw them into the brush where they broke on the rocks beneath. The flames quickly rose to the treetops. From down under the smoke, the disciples had a clear view of the village.

As the fire spread, the people began running from their shelters in every direction. As they did, they were cut down by the disciples. The smell of flesh being cooked from the bone filled the air as many of the people were set ablaze. The smoke was so thick that it choked the life out of any who found themselves lost in its dark maze of searing heat and pain.

In this swirling darkness of death the disciples chose to meet the Warrior for what would be a test that the Warrior and his people were not prepared to meet .

Arrow after arrow added to the scene of complete terror. Fire and smoke engulfed everything, and the bodies of both young and old were burning. The Warrior was now torn between saving all those he had come to know and killing the disciples before there was no one left to save. The first signs of weakness appeared, and there was no way to take them away. The Warrior was unable to kill the disciples without being distracted by the ones he now cared for being burned.

The disciples were correct in their tactic, for it served its purpose. The Warrior was now fighting the disciples not only for his life, but also his own mind for his sanity in the midst of evil unleashed and directed at him. It was almost more than he could take.

At that moment he did the only thing he could—he invoked his power. The warrior knew that not only the disciples but also many of the people would be killed by the shock wave. If he hesitated for much longer, then all the people would perish. It was a hard choice to make, but it had already been made by the disciples.

The moment before he unleashed the finality of his decision, the Medicine Man knew that the Warrior was left with no choice but to act. He had always wanted to see the boy happy, but this would not happen. He had hoped that the boy knew that he was sorry for doing these things the people thought were necessary. How were the ones who lived across the river any worse?

The Warrior saw out of the corner of his eye the Medicine Man with in the range of the shock wave, but he knew he could wait no longer. In that moment their eyes met; in the next the Medicine Man was torn apart by the force of the Warrior's power.

The disciples witnessed this just before they too shared the same fate, along with many of the people. The fire was put out, and a stillness rang loud, so loud it was the only thing that could be heard—not the screams, not the cries, just the deafening quiet that even the Warrior could hear, and he wished he were dreaming.

Without the Medicine Man to help the Warrior adjust to his new life, much of it had not been what the Warrior had thought it would be. He felt an urgency or an uneasiness at times as he tried to become one of the people.

It wasn't at the times one would expect either. It wasn't at the moments before battle or when the people were removing the dead men that he had killed from the battlefield, which was also the people's home. Or as he walked to the place where the dried meat was stored to fetch himself a meal. The same place where Drone had killed the old woman, unleashing the sickness into the people's home. The same sickness that made him necessary.

It was during the moments of everyday life—those are what turned in his stomach. That's when he would think of what it was that bothered him. The reason! The reason for all of this. This pain and this fear and even for him. That reason is why he was necessary.

Drone had infected the land and its people, and that is why he was there. Not because he was wanted. He did not arrive in joy with the welcome of all. No, not him. He was there with the people because he was necessary. Maybe the rest were brought forth in love or happiness, but he was not. He had come to the people for a reason. He was born for a purpose. They were both necessary, and they were both the same.

The Warrior was there in the people's home to kill men! To be the cure for the sickness Drone had brought to the people. The Warrior could not understand how the cure for the sickness was the sickness itself.

The Warrior thought of not only Drone but also of Teeosh. If Teeosh had not tried to escape from her work, then he would not be alive or better yet, necessary. He was by no means alive. He could remember all the men that he had killed and the reason he had done this.

It wasn't the Commander that had brought the sickness; it was Teeosh that had offered herself to the Commander, once again not wanting to pay what was owed. Teeosh said that the Commander had called her his child, had she not? What father would not put his hands on his child if it would stop the child from being killed.

Had Teeosh not tempted the Commander when she was being corrected? The Commander said that Drone was a reminder of a moment of weakness forever. Was it not the Warrior's own mother that had called the hunters? They themselves carried both Drone and his mother back into the people's home along with the sickness.

A great celebration had begun, is how it was told to the ones who were not there, the ones that came after. Drone was infected with the sickness, but still his mother had brought him, putting herself before the rest of the people. The guilt she carried was because of those choices, causing many more to die before the people would pay what was owed.

While looking through the hole in his hut, he realized that nothing was familiar from outside of those stone walls. He sat up in the darkness. He had chosen to stay in his hut because the heat of a fire made him uneasy. It was cold, and his breath could be seen in the air. He motioned to the darkness.

"I have come to this place on my own," he said as he slammed his foot down to the ground. "I have chosen to walk this road." These words were the Warrior's own declaration of war. "Men have come to the people's home and brought war. I have no purpose except what I was born into. Into pain I was born, and out of pain I will go. Know that when I do go, I will take many more with me."

It was early, and the sun had not yet peeked over the face of the mountain that held the people's home in its shadows. Darkness was a place he knew to be safe. In the dark he was home, and it seemed to breathe for him.

He began before the daylight had reached down to wake the people from their sleep. With him he took only his spear; it held an obsidian blade that was as sharp as any iron. He took many stone knives, as well as a stone ax.

Across his face where his eyes could be seen, he smeared

the black war paint of soot and snake venom. It burned his face, but the Warrior was use to pain. Once he had gathered what would be needed, the Warrior began in his attempt to serve his purpose and to be remembered.

The air was cold, and dew covered the long grasses on the meadow that led down to the river. As he reached the water, he could see off a ways by the light of a small fire two women talking.

The women could sense the Warrior's eyes on them, so they began to look out into the darkness. As they peered into the shadows, his armor reflected the moon's light, and the women could just make out his form against the night sky.

The sight of him caused the women to gasp. It was a reaction that many of the people had whenever they were caught off guard by him. He seemed to always be lurking off in obscure shadows or in places seldom noticed by the others. He waited for a moment longer, before walking straight into the water as he began to cross the river to the other side.

He had been told stories of a man who could be an ally in his fight. He was a man whose thirst for revenge was never quenched. He would no doubt be hunting off near the Thunder Mountains.

As the Warrior reached the shore of the land of rock and thorn, he could see the evidence of soldiers. He began north in the direction of the hazy sky that hung over an ancient volcano. As he moved, he noticed more evidence of soldiers, until something caught his eye.

Many soldiers moving along the ridge of the foothills. The

soldiers were traveling in the same direction as him, and he was sure that none of them would see their destination.

They pushed slaves that were tied to long poles. All of these people were very weak, and the soldiers were relentlessly pushing them to move.

The Warrior followed behind the soldiers just out of view, although it seemed as if these men traveled without worry of attack. Their attention was on the slaves or on their own conversations with one another. None of their eyes scanned the land.

Smoke and heat came up from cracks in the earth, making it very hot. Jagged stones covered the ground, providing scorpions with hiding places where they huddled together as they attempted to avoid the blistering heat, as well as the vipers that slithered about everywhere.

The Warrior was gaining on the soldiers when he noticed movement up ahead. Boneface Warriors appeared from out of a rocky canyon. These men were very cautious as they approached the soldiers, but it wasn't the soldiers that they seemed to be on the lookout for. The men exchanged a few gestures as the people that were tied to the long poles were handed over to the Boneface. The Boneface continued north as they quickly rushed their captives into the canyon while keeping their eyes to the surrounding landscape. Unlike the soldiers, none of the Boneface spoke as they moved through the barren wasteland.

The Warrior followed close behind the soldiers when again he noticed movement off in the direction that the Boneface had gone in. There, on a cluster of rocks, was a man moving around just above the narrow trail that led into the canyon.

The man traversed the hot walls of the canyon as if he were an insect, able to find a grip in the smallest of spaces. He moved silently just above the Boneface.

His light armor made of thin stones had been shaped to fit his body so that it was the perfect camouflage. The man needed only to remain still, and he would instantly disappear into the landscape. This man was no doubt the cause of the Boneface's worry and also the reason that the Warrior had chosen to travel north.

The Boneface pushed their captives at a brutal pace, and still the man above on the rock walls kept up with the group. The Warrior also followed close behind, finding it more difficult to stay out of the view of the Boneface.

Suddenly the group stopped, as the one that led them held his fist in the air. In a dead tree that stood off to the right of the trail was a grizzly sign that had been set for these men. There hanging from a tree were dozens of Boneface hands that had been removed from their owners. It was a chilling sign set by the Spider. A warning to the Boneface that they were being hunted.

Suddenly the Warrior misjudged his footing, sending a rock tumbling down. The sound of the rock hitting against other rocks caused the Boneface to suddenly stop, exchanging looks with one another.

The Warrior crouched down behind a large stone. The Boneface stood still for only a moment as ants began to sting the men where they stood. At once they all started in the direction of the sound. Each one holding a spear above his head, moving in a single-file line through the narrow corridor of the canyon.

These men all wore an armor of human bones. Partly ornamental and partly purposeful. A testament to their brutality. Their spears twisted by fire and their teeth sharpened to points. Boneface were known to drop their weapons in battle if they came upon an unarmed foe, using only their teeth while swarming a man, eating him alive on the battlefield. A gruesome display of cannibalism that earned them their dreadful reputation.

As the Boneface came to the large stone that concealed the Warrior, one motioned with his hand so that the others would split the group in two, and approach from either side of the rock. He was sure that this would be the end of the man that had victimized them since many of them were young boys.

He thought of how his name would be remembered forever as a legend. The Boneface that killed Ten Hands the Spider. The thought alone caused him to raise up a little higher as he tried on his new fame in his head. That's when he noticed that none of the warriors had gone past him on either side. He could hear the sound of fingernails scraping the rock wall as limbs banged against it. The Boneface were trying to free themselves as they were pulled high up onto the wall by the man above.

The last Boneface couldn't decide which way to run, causing his feet to shudder, running straight into the rock, knocking him to the ground. From his back he could see hanging from the stonewall the bodies of the other Boneface. He jumped back to his feet and turned to run. That's when he found the Warrior's blade, killing him as the two men came eye to eye.

"I know who you are," said the Spider as he hung just out

of reach, wiping fresh blood from his knife. "What are you here for?" the Spider asked. The Warrior pushed forward with his head toward the fallen Boneface. "I see. Well, there's a lot more of them, and if we get tired of Boneface, there's plenty of soldiers to put into the ground." The Warrior gave a slight nod to show he agreed.

"What happened? How did you get like this?" The Warrior just stared, not speaking. "So, it's true. Your people did this to you?" The Spider could see that the Warrior was different than any man he had ever known. "You don't talk? Well I hope you don't mind if I do. I haven't had anyone to talk to for a long time, said the Spider, as he hung from the wall upside down. He was relaxed as he continued speaking, looking down at the Warrior. I can't say that I know how you feel. I did have good times, but that was long ago. I know what it's like to be alone. It hurts bad until it doesn't, I remember that. Once that pain leaves you and you're numb, you're able to breathe again. That's relief until you realize you haven't felt anything for so long you almost want that pain, to feel again, but you can't.

"That's even worse than being alone. You forget everything before, even the good. Without that you lose who you were and become someone that is a stranger. All that's left is the bleakness, and home is a mystery. Looks like you already know this place. So, if that's what we have left, let's go together and welcome the next."

This time would be known as the reckoning of thorns, a bloody summer that would be remembered in the land of rock and thorn forever. The tide changed that day, and the men of violence finally knew what it was like to run for their lives.

That summer was spent in a nonstop down pour of both Boneface, and soldiers blood. That summer was spent in a nonstop down pour of both Bonefac, and soldiers blood. Attack after attack finally sent the Boneface back underground. The caves that served as their entrances into the vast underground tunnels were sealed up early in the season. The Boneface were unable to make proper preparations for the winter, causing many to die of starvation.

The soldiers also took heavy casualties at the hands of the two men; they seemed to be around every corner, as well as in every shadow. Men were left in piles along every road. It seemed no matter how the soldiers prepared for these attacks, it was never enough to stop the Spider and the Warrior.

The soldiers found themselves running through the dark, screaming as they tripped over their own feet, only to find their way right into the blades of the ones they were trying to escape from.

Many soldiers had abandoned their post during this time, leaving the lands that the warlords ruled, open to attack. Stables, along with an armory, were burned to the ground, causing the people under the warlords' rule to riot in objection to their rulers' inability to stop the attacks.

When the summer was finally over, the Spider and the Warrior parted ways satisfied in their attempts to be remembered by the ones that ruled the land of rock and thorn.

CHAPTER 10

With the Medicine Man gone and the people nearly completely destroyed, every family had suffered the loss of at least one. Still others were left without a single family member alive. The people were now introduced to a place they had never known, left on the doorstep to the reality of war.

It was as if the people could not see who they had once been. The ones who should have been there to remind them were all gone.

Those empty pieces were needed to fill in the picture of who the people were. It seemed that the tribe would not recover. Their sadness was all that was left, and when they believed that they could take no more, they found that they would have to.

The morning of the first rain of the season, the Warrior died. He died for many reasons, but most of all, because he was alone. The Warrior had taken a wife, and she had been with child. That child had been lost during the attack by the Blood Disciples—or so he thought.

The Medicine Man and Sutkey were both gone. The things that the Warrior had witnessed and been forced to do finally overtook him.

When this happened, the rest of the people fell to the

ground. No one had the strength to stand. As they did, the Warrior's wife felt a great pain in her body, and out came a child.

The child was the Warriors daughter. Even though he was gone, he had left her in his place so that she would be the one to protect his people. That was why they called her Supal, "The One."

She lay there in her mother's arms, and the people began to stand. They began to walk off in the direction of the newest member of the tribe. They touched her and introduced themselves. They all welcomed the child, but not one would look at her. On that day, she was born, the greatest warrior.

With the warrior gone, it was nearly the end of the people. If not for the child, all hope would have been lost. The people would have ceased to exist. Even with her, some felt that there was no hope. How could a child protect them? Even more, how could a girl? It was true her father was the Warrior, but with no Medicine Man to teach her, there was no reason to think she would be able to protect the people.

Many believed she would be nothing like her father. They were right, but not in the way that they had thought. So many had left the village in retreat, in hopes of being spared by the soldiers. Many more pieces were taken from the now shapeless picture that had once been the tribe. So many that it could not be recognized.

Many concerns were true. However, they did not put a wager on this child so that they could profit from her ability. No they put faith in her because, that was what war did not take, and could not take—hope for the future. If that were lost, then the Warrior would have died for nothing.

That was not the way of the people. The Warrior died so that they could live, and that was what they would do.

They would live in the face of soldiers, in the face of all who would have them die, for they had no choice. The Warrior had not chosen to have the life he was given. The life he lived was chosen for him, and he in turn chose theirs.

They were alive because he fought and saved them from certain death. So they must live. Little did they know that she would be the greatest warrior that the people would ever know.

Eventually, the village was rebuilt but without the Warrior and without so many of the people who were once part of their life, it was hard for the tribe to repair what had been lost.

■ ■ ■

When the Commander received word of the disciples' defeat, a rage overtook him. A need for revenge consumed him, as he now felt that the people would pay, no matter what the cost. The Commander started at once rebuilding the army that he had lost, taking in men from the surrounding lands, costing him nearly all that he had left in gold.

It included more than double the men, as well as beasts from over the sea—beasts that could not be stopped. He also was able to acquire Barak eagles at an extremely high price, and even though the price was great, these killers of the sky were highly effective.

Still, the Commander's hatred for the tribe burned inside his heart. He would visit every village and every town in the land of rock and thorn. He welcomed any and all able-bodied men from both his lands, which were the same ones that his father had been raised up in from birth, and also all the surrounding lands.

At sunrise the men were awakened by the sound of the horns being blown, to let them all know it was time to move. The Commander had been going over tactics with his higher-ranking men all night. He received word that the Warrior had died, and at this news, he was relieved. Something inside of him held on to this fear of the Warrior. He had to overcome, he told himself. He would not make the same mistake as he had last time. The men were to be the best he had ever known.

Their days were spent training until they moved as if they were one. Time seemed to stand still as the commander was eager to put his men to the test. It would be many more years before he would once again step foot on the people's land. With every passing day, the fire grew, and his rage was more than any man could ever control.

■ ■ ■

As the girl grew, she was never told of her father or the Medicine Man. So, after many years had passed, she still did not know the truth. She was a joyful child, but like many of the children, she was without a father and longed to know who he was. When she would ask her mother, she would simply reply, "Someday child, but not on this day," and that would remain her answer for many years. As the girl grew she began to replace him with dance. She moved through the village, dancing around as she worked, twirling and leaping, all the while humming a tune all her own. She rarely walked, and this brought much joy to her heart.

Then one day, as she was busy at work, she overheard a boy say, "Is that her? Is that the Warrior's daughter?" She saw the boy looking in her direction, and when she turned her head to look behind her, there was no one else.

This brought in her a strange feeling, so once again she approached her mother with a question. Only this time, it was different.

"Mother," Supal said.

"Yes."

"Who is the Warrior?" she asked; Supal could see the expression on her mother's face drift to another place.

"Who told you of this person?" her mother asked; she clearly had not expected to hear the name and was caught off guard by her daughter's question.

"I heard a boy today as I worked down by the oak trees. He said that I was the Warrior's daughter. Is it true? Who is he, and why is he called the Warrior?" she asked.

With that, her mother sat her down and produced writings that had belonged to the Medicine Man. In those writings was the entire story of who the Warrior was and how he had come to be. When they had finally heard the story, the two held each other and cried.

"Why did the people do those things to my father?" she asked.

"Because it was necessary, or so we thought. He was needed, so it was decided that it was to be him, your father," her mother replied.

"But he must have lived his life feeling so lonely. He must have felt like nobody cared." Then a worried look came across Supal's face. "Who taught him to dance?" she asked.

"Dance?" her mother asked. "I don't believe he ever did dance," she replied.

With this statement, she understood her daughter's look, and again they both cried. She spent the next days asking the older ones who had been there, questions about her father. Each person was relieved to finally be able to express their gratefulness and ask for forgiveness. It weighed heavily on the hearts of all. They all told their story of how the Warrior had changed their lives forever, and of the events that they had seen.

Soon a sad picture had formed in the girl's mind.

"Is that why so many of the people left?" asked Supal.

"No, I don't believe so. It was because your father had passed, and some did not believe that you would be able to protect the people," her mother continued.

"Protect the people? Why me?"

"Because you are of his bloodline, the bloodline of the Warrior. We believe that it was not only the people who chose the Warrior, but the Creator as well. We believe this because of the things he did. These things can only be done in the light of the one who is light, the Creator. Also, who else will teach your father to dance?"

"How can I teach him to dance now?"

"Because he is still here. He sees you. He is in the wind, in the trees, and he is in all you see. That is how you can teach him to dance."

Those words gave in her a new hope. She could feel him, her father, the one they called the Warrior. She began to move to a different dance, one she had never known, and she knew it was because he was dancing with her.

Even though the people could not see him, they who had been there all knew that dance. It was as if he had returned, still in battle against those who had come to harm the people. As they looked on, they fell to the ground and raised their hands to the sky. They all thanked the Creator for the child as their own doubts were washed away. They knew that the hopes that they had for her would be so.

Once the dance was over, all the people gathered, and they led her to the mound in the center of the village. They told her that this was where he had lived and that this was where they had laid his body down for the last time. Then, without warning, she ordered them to bring two large logs to where they stood.

Once they were brought, she had them fasten them together to form a perch and place it atop the mound. Then she said these words: "As the ravens cast their lot, let it be known that the Warrior has returned," and with that, she leaped atop the perch and so prepared to start her training. That day would be the last time anyone would see her face. She would keep it covered so that only her eyes could be seen. Her eyes were as black as the raven's wing, with hair to match, as if a dark river flowed over her body. It was clear to all that not only the spirit of the Warrior but also the raven had entered her so that she would be known to the people and would be called the Blackbird. To future generations, she would be known as "The

Greatest Warrior," for that is what she became. It all happened with a dance.

■ ■ ■

As time passed Supal was able to study the writings and began to train. She would train by day and study by the light of a small fire at night, and it was during this time that she discovered when the Commander's hate for the people had first begun. She learned what all the people had already known.

She had found out that the Medicine Man's father had been a soldier. He had been found on the people's side of the river, washed up on the shore after a terrible storm. He had been nursed to health by the people and also had fallen in love with a woman of the tribe. They had been very much in love. Soon they were joined as one in the ways of the people.

After a brief time, they became with child. It was a joyful time for all. The soldier was very much loved by all the tribe. Suddenly the Medicine Man's mother became extremely sick. The baby, it seemed, would not make it. In that moment she chose to give up her life so that the child would live. The soldier had begged her not to do this. He had promised that they would someday have another child, but she would have nothing to do with this. She did what she felt she must, and the Medicine Man was born. The people were torn between the joy for the child and the sorrow for the loss of his mother, but none more than the soldier. Without his wife, he was unable to care for the child now that his heart was broken, so he left the boy in the care of the tribe and returned to the land of rock and thorn, never to return.

After some time he was once again joined to a woman, but she could never replace the one who had been lost. Again, he had a child, and he was to be the one that the tribe would come to know as the Commander. The Commander had known of his half-brother from the other side of the river as his father often talked of the regret that he had for leaving the boy. Many times he had become drunk and had spoken too freely of his love for the boy that he had left behind.

Soon the Commander began to hide a hate that grew inside for the brother he did not know. He had dreamed that he would one day meet him in battle. He would imagine himself defeating his brother in front of their father. Then his father would see that he too was worthy of his love. It was only the hope of a child for the love of his father. As he grew, his hate also grew, and as the soldier lay on his deathbed, the boy made a vow that he would do this very thing—all for what he saw as the robbery of his father's love by one he did not know.

So that was how the Commander had come to hate the people, and that was something that Supal did not understand. So, she would continue to study the writings for some type of answer that she hoped was there. As Supal read the last pages of the Medicine Man's writings about her father, she saw that the words had changed. She realized these pages were in the Warrior's own words, which the Medicine Man had written. He had left these behind so that he could someday be known. This is when she found what she had been hoping to find. It said that at the age of eight years, he had become aware of things that had changed him. From the center of them all was where he had watched them over the years, and even if they never looked at him, it did not mean that he had not been watching them all along. He knew them without ever saying a word. He knew them better than they knew themselves. He had seen everything that they had ever done. Since they had never looked at him, it was easy to forget that he was even there. They had walked by him on the way back from the river during the hottest days of the summer, carrying cool water so that they all could be refreshed. Never did one stop to offer him a drink. There had been so many celebrations, but never had they considered allowing him to join in the memories. The Warrior would watch them as they danced, and he would dance alone, using his best manners when asking a young lady to dance, even if there was no one really there. It was just him alone in the space that was his entire world. All these things were not real, but in his mind, they were all having a wonderful time. He was just like the rest, and it was great. He was careful not to step on anyone's toes in the small space, which was dark, with not even the moonlight to cast a shadow for company.

In his mind he felt like he knew them all. He had run with the boys on there way to the river, jumping and laughing. He would sometimes wait the entire day to share a treat with a special someone, even if they never knew it.

Many were just as much a part of the boy's life as Turtle. It was at night when the village was quiet that his tears would sometimes fall. That was why Turtle was so much more than just a turtle. He was the only one there when the boy had no one else. He remembered that he had watched the children swim an entire morning. It had been so hot, and he had been standing most of that morning on the tips of his toes. He could see them all through a small hole that he had pushed out the side of his hut. He imagined that he was also there, jumping up and down in his hut, pretending to splash water at them as he laughed. No one had ever looked at him besides the Medicine Man. He had always believed that he was invisible to the rest of the people. On this day everything changed.

One of the younger children had strayed away from the rest, and none had noticed. He watched the child wander away from the others, slipping on a wet rock, rolling into a deep pool without a sound. The child struggled to find a grip on the slippery stones.. The Warrior freed himself from his hut, running to where the boy was. He quickly grabbed hold of the child, pulling him onto the shore. It was what the boy did next that changed the Warrior's life. The boy had smiled at him, touching his face before walking back to the others. This was when the Warrior realized that he could be seen, and that the others had just chosen not to look at him. Until the day the Medicine Man explained to him his reason for being, it had always hurt so very much. Once he understood what had happened, he accepted it, believing it was his destiny.

Like her father, she also believed it was her destiny to protect her people. She would do it the only way she knew how, with everything she had.

She would look to the Black Scrolls to help her on the battlefield. Not only those, but she would also look to the Medicine Mans writings. They told the whole story of her father and his fate. To live alone, to fight alone, and in the end, to die alone.

As she trained, she could feel him there with her. Day after day the beat of the drums grew louder and louder. With every boom, with every leap and thrust, every time her heart would beat in her chest, she was teaching him to dance. A dance to the song that would be written in blood, the blood of those who doubted that she lived her destiny for her father, the Warrior. When the day came for her to serenade her enemy, they would all know that she was the Warrior's daughter.

The dance was a combination of powerful jumps and rolls, all put together for the purpose of war. Supal began with her head looking down to the earth. Her long black hair fell loosely to her side. The drummers took hold of the sky as they all began with the beat, slowly at first, every man coming down in perfect unison with the others, gentle but steady as her arms started to rise from where they hung at her side, almost despite her, as her head seemed to follow her arms to the steady beat. Up and down, over and over, until her feet also seemed to come under the spell of the music. First the right, then the left. They were weightless as they floated up, then suddenly slammed back down to the earth with the force of the people's defiance for those who would bring harm to the tribe. She held to her connection to the sky, as she was able to elevate herself to unnatural heights by invoking her power, which was branded to her in pain as the sign of those who had passed.

As word spread throughout the land of the Warrior's victory, as well as his death, the other tribes started to ask themselves questions that they had never asked before.

"What if that had been us?" A young hunter brought before the people.

His concern was a good one, as many others also felt the same. This was the Wolf tribe of the flatlands just beyond the river. Also, the Bear tribe of the desert found themselves asking the very same questions. Had it not been for the Warrior, the sickness could have come to them as well. So it was decided that they too would offer up one of their own.

The Wolf tribe were tall people who lived in the plains. They had always been a peaceful people, hunting buffalo and were renowned for being able to run from sun to sun without stopping. Stealth was their most formidable ability. It was said that they could touch a man's nose on a clear day and be gone without being seen.

"What can we do? If we do not prepare for the soldiers, then we are nothing more than a bird without wings. Next to fill the snake's belly." The people of the Wolf all agreed that they would do their part, sending one of their own to aid the Blackbird in this fight.

The Bear tribe of the desert were a strong and powerful people. Able to lift as much as five men. They carried large rocks a great distance, creating man-made rock crops. Small animals of many types would seek shelter there, and this would provide them with their main food source.

These people lived in underground caves that they dug out of the sand. They spent most of their days asleep because of the hot desert climate and at night they were often thought to be ghosts because of their light complexions.

"We have heard that the Wolf have joined the Blackbird in the hopes of stopping the soldiers from spreading their murder. Now I can only speak for myself, but I believe that the Bear should also send one to help defend our home. Let us choose the one who can prove that he may stand alongside the Wolf and the Blackbird."

"You have visitors," said one of the hunters as he entered the box canyon. It had been set aside so that it could serve as her personal battlefield.

The Blackbird had been training but stopped quickly asking, "Who?"

She was breathing heavily as sweat fell from her head.

"It is old ones from the Wolf, as well as the Bear."

"What is it that they are here for?" asked Supal.

"They claim that after this day you will fight no more alone, for they have brought a young man from each of them to aid you in the protection of our people," he replied.

"I don't know what to do as far as teaching them to be warriors," she said as she tried to catch her breath.

"The Black Scrolls should do fine for that," answered the hunter.

"Well, let's meet them" she said, motioning to her drummers to stop for a moment.

The hunter left and quickly returned with the two boys.

"Thank you," Supal said to the hunter. With that he was gone, leaving her with the new offerings from the Wolf and the Bear clan.

"Hello," she said.

"Hello," said the boy from the Bear.

"I am Turak."

Then it was the boy from the Wolf's turn.

"Hello, we are Wha and Tru," said the boy from the Wolf. "Wait. What did you say" she asked.

"We are Wah and Tru." "That is strange because as you speak, I hear two voices."

"That is because we are two boys," the one in front of her said.

Again she heard two voices.

"I don't understand," and then from behind the boy came another boy. They were identical to each other.

"Oh, twins!" she said with a look of surprise.

"Yes, we are twins," they both said together.

"It's amazing, but I see no difference at all between you."

"That's because there is none," said the boys, and as she looked, she could see that this was true. The two of them were tall, lean boys with long black hair. They had muscular bodies and a look of contentment in their eyes.

"So, tell me about yourselves," said Supal.

"What do you want to know?" the boys said, again at the same time.

"Why are you here?" she asked.

"We are here so that you will teach us to be warriors like your father. We wish to show you that our people care about our home and that your father is missed by us as well. We are here to give our lives so that you live and so the warrior will never be forgotten."

"Why would you do this" she asked.

"Because of what the Warrior did for us" they answered.

Next was the boy from the Bear.

"You, Turak. What about you?"

"What do you want to know?" the boy asked.

"What can you do?"

"I can lift heavy things, and I can break things that are strong, like rocks and other men's wills," said Turak.

"Let us see. What about me?"

"What do you mean?" asked Turak. He was not sure what she was asking him.

"Try to grab me and hold me down. Make me laugh if you think you can."

"I don't think that would be very hard since you are a girl," said Turak.

"If you say so, lets just hope you never have to see what this girl can do" she said.

Supal could remember the twins words as she laid her head down that night. "Because of what he did for us." It was true, her father did what he did for all. He did not do what he did for any one person. It was a selfless act that he expected nothing in return, except to be seen. He hoped then he could be accepted. Without Turtle he had nothing, so he fought for a chance to be seen by anyone.

Her training would be different than before with three new men who had been offered by their people. First were the twin brothers Wah, and Tru of the Wolf tribe along with Turak of the Bear.

Both Wah and Tru were tall boys, two years younger than Supal. They both carried curved blades the length of their arms that could be swung with power. They were men of few words, eager to make their tribe proud in the choice they had made in them.

Turak was not as tall as the twins but was built as solid as an oak tree. His strength was unbelievable as he was able to pick up exceptionally large things. In the tug-of-war it took ten men to move him an inch. He carried a mighty war club that he had made himself.

All these men would prove to be especially useful on the battlefield. So, the four of them would train together.

As they began their training, they found four drummers to accompany the four that Supal already had to help with the dance.

"What would you have us do?" they asked.

She ordered them to listen carefully. Then she instructed them on how to fasten large drums together along with what materials they would need. "When you have completed this task, return to me" she instructed.

They quickly got to work preparing the drums to be made

at specific sizes, one larger than the next, and also the depths to control the boom they would create.

Supal and the others trained as taught in the Black Scrolls. At night she would go over the Medicine Man's writings. She had learned that he had once been one of the Blood Disciples. This had been when he first crossed over the river, so long ago. This is when he had taken the Black Scrolls —all these teachings intact and complete. There were great instructions and detail in the ancient ways of battle. All created over generations with proven tactics of war. Many of these were old texts thought to have been lost but were now found. In them was everything she would need to help her.

Once the drums were completed, she instructed the men in the beat that the dance was to be fought in. She and the others trained in a box canyon that was her private battlefield. She was sure it had been created by the very winds that now cooled her face.

She started with her body stiff, without a curved line in it. Then in another moment, she seemed to turn awkwardly before bending back to the way she had begun. With every boom, her movements becoming fluid and natural, taking on the appearance of a raven in flight. With that movement coming to a natural place of ease, the girl raised her head up, leaping from her perch. Instead of down, she went up, and then with another stride, a little higher and higher until she was looking down from the top of the canyon walls.

She chose the strongest porcupine quills to use as throwing weapons. They were smeared in the deadly poison of the red and yellow tree frogs that could be found high in the treetops.

The quills were extraordinarily strong and could be thrown with deadly accurate skill from above.

Soon a hunter interrupted her once again. "I have news" he said.

"They began arriving two days ago," he continued as Supal gave him her full attention.

"What are they?" she asked.

"I don't know, but they are carried by the wind and seem to be for you,"

"For me?" Supal asked with a puzzled look on her face.

"They carry the mark of both you and your father," he said, pointing to small marks that had been scratched on the out side of the pods. Suddenly they began to notice that the pods seemed to be humming. One of the drummers looked as if he had something to say, but in his rush to speak, his words were lost for a moment.

"Speak boy. What is it?" asked the Blackbird.

"Spiral trees, that's what they are," said the boy.

"How do you know this?" the hunter asked.

"I just do. That's how the tribes of before used to get word to one another."

With this statement, their memory was refreshed, and they all could recall stories that were the same as he had said.

The Blackbird took one of the spiral trees' buds in her hand. With her touch, it started to open, revealing a message that had been placed inside.

"We the people of our grandfathers and ambassadors to the eagles of the Rim Cloud, Companions of the Light. Send word on this day with an offering of two eagles of the Rim

Cloud as well as Sequel, son of Theous. He is a brother in our duty, as overseers of the Rim Cloud. They await your arrival so that they may accompany you to their new home."

They all stood there, as another one opened, and it read.

"With all of our intent to be laid out before you, and to answer your request. We offer our champion, Two-Chop, as he is known to us. Able to fall a tree with only two swings of his ax. For the rest of our days, may your name be held in high regard."

"Another one is opening" said the hunter. He was speaking of another one of the spiral tree buds that had been brought by the wind.

"To answer your request in the way you have instructed, here awaiting the daughter of our protector, the Warrior, is our most beloved. Although young, the power has descended. From atop their shoulders it has given them the ability of foresight, dominion over the small and many, along with the one who speaks in the ancient language. In high tones she spoke in this tongue so that she was heard in the midst of the Great Storm. These three came as one. In love, they shall remain as one. Our only wish is that they live to serve the Blackbird, as her name was also called by the one who is all. This to complete the foreseen time of thunder, steel, and armor."

"The foreseen time of thunder, steel, and armor? What does it all mean?" said the Blackbird with a look of confusion.

"It means that the Medicine Man prepared help for you,"

"Help with what?" she asked, and she wondered what it all meant.

"Help with something that is of great importance," replied one of the old ones with a reassuring look on his face.

Then the last one opened, bringing the final offering of Ten Hands the Spider. "I am, as you are, the center of our people, last of the tribe of the Great Cave people, ten hands and ten blades of stone, awaiting your return to me and preparing our stronghold. I have come to know your father in this life, and it would be my honor to also know you."

"What now?" asked the Blackbird.

"Maybe we should go get them," said the boy called Wah.

"Maybe we should," she agreed.

"It would take nearly a season to travel to all these places and back, and it worried her to be gone so long from home. If the Medicine Man had thought it was necessary, she could not wait another moment.

The twins, Turak, and the Blackbird prepared to travel the long way across the land to the Sky Rim and even beyond.

"My people, please know that my heart hurts that we will be apart for this time. Every part of me is us. We go to return the children to their place. A place of honor. To the front. Know that on that day a line will be drawn. A line that can only be crossed in brotherhood or stopped with force."

They had been traversing the foothills that led onto a vast plain. Up ahead, a grove of willow trees stood on either side of an old hunters trail, that they had been traveling on. It seemed that they had walked for days when they heard what sounded like water flowing with the force of a river.

"Do you hear that?" said Turak as they all stopped where they stood, listening to the sound.

The sound was so loud they could not move. A rumble also came, and soon the ground started to shake. Then without warning, from out of the trees came wild horses.

"Move!" shouted Supal, nearly being trampled by the horses. A white stallion led the group. His mane flowing in the wind that was caused by his powerful legs. His coat was white, without a spot or flaw. The Blackbird knew that it would be him, she would ride into battle.

"Did you see the white one in the front ?" asked Turak. "It was a spirit horse that just entered this world. The horse who carries the pure of heart, a warhorse of swift judgment." What should we do now?" said Wah.

"Nothing, just wait," Supal answered.

The group found a comfortable place to wait. It was a cold night, and the group remained still. They heard a noise ahead in the darkness at the edge of the moonlight. There stood the spirit horse, steam coming from his nostrils with every breath. The Blackbird and the horse locked eyes, and she began to speak in the language of all living things. As she did, her heart began to beat so hard all could hear it, or so she thought.

"I am your sister in the fight to free this land of all who would have it destroyed; that is why I'm asking for your help. Help us to retrieve our brothers in this fight."

Then he walked closer and then closer; finally her hand was on his face. They would be one in their purpose, never demanding but always free.

The brothers chose to walk and run, since their endurance was great. Turak was given a brown male horse slightly larger than most, and the journey would be much faster. Soon the

Sky Rim was in sight—sheer cliffs shooting straight up and into the clouds.

"What are you going up there for?" asked Turak. A gate led into a narrow canyon that started up and into the mountain.

"Well, I was just thinking that maybe they could come down and see us."

"What's wrong, Turak, scared of high places?" Supal asked.

"I just like to stay on ground that's below the clouds, that's all."

"Then wait here and guard our back."

"I can do that," said Turak, relieved by the suggestion.

They had traveled for two days, and soon they had doubt that they would find their way there or would even be able to get off the mountain alive. It was wrong turn after wrong turn until they were not even sure where it was that they had started from. When almost all hope had been lost, they saw a small fire up ahead.

"A fire" one of the twins said.

"Well, if that's it, then we will make it; if not, then we may need to turn back," said Supal.

The last part of the hike was in a thick fog since it was well into the clouds. A shadow appeared on the ground just ahead of their feet.

"What was that?" said one of the twins.

Then the shadow came again, and it was clearly a large eagle.

"Did you see that?" asked Wah.

"Quiet—it's hunting!" Supal answered as she dropped to the ground.

With that, the boys also fell to the ground, keeping their eyes to the sky.

"Hunting for what?" whispered Wah.

Just then, as if to answer the question, the eagle fell into a dive. With its wings held back, it dropped faster and faster. At the last moment, it changed direction, claws stretched out, grabbing a goat that none of them had seen standing on the high mountain walls. The eagle then pulled it from the narrow ledge and out into space, letting it go. The goat and the eagle understood this event, the goat with an acceptance of it, a respect for the other's life.

"Did you see that? It was like it was planned, the way they looked at each other," said Wah.

The eagle landed on the ground and began to eat his meal. That's when the four were able to get an idea of how big the eagle was. He was massive, with claws that were perfectly shaped for cutting into flesh, his beak as well.

"So you think we're bringing two of those back with us? OK, but I hope that they know that," said one of the boys.

Then from out of the corner of their eyes, they noticed a man standing near an old tree.

"Hello," said Supal. "I am—" she started to say.

"I know who you are. I've been waiting for you," said the man.

"How do you know who I am?" Supal thought it was strange that the man would know who she was.

"I knew you when we were still in the time before, when we were still in the land of our ancestors, but that was another life and another time. What I meant was I know who you are,"

Sequel said in a kind and welcoming way. "But the question is, do you?"

"What do you mean?" she asked as another eagle landed on top of the tree beside them.

"The one—do you know what that means?" he asked.

"Yes, I am the Warrior's daughter, protector of my people. So, they call me 'The One.'

"I see, but I am Sequel. I will also be a protector of your people. That is why you are here at Sky Rim, correct? The ones with you are also here to help in this event."

"Event? What do you mean event? This is forever, for all of our life until the next ones come to take our place," said Supal.

"Now I see that you truly do not know who you are. You are the last and the beginning. None come after you. Everything starts and ends with you—the one chance we all have to preserve ourselves. It is not me or I, but us, and that is where love lives. If you forget that, then we have already lost. Are you ready?" Sequel asked.

"Ready for what?"

"To save your people, not only them but all people of this world. As we speak, the two-legged beast has returned. He means to stop you from doing this. Your name is on his lips, and he will never stop until you, and all of us are dead, until there is nowhere that love can be in this place that is our home. The time is here; the lot has been cast. The last battle for this time is now."

His words hit hard at the hearts of those who were there. The twins and the Blackbird knew in their spirit it was all true. Then Supal asked, "How do you know this?"

Hearing her question, he glanced at the eagle atop the tree and said, "A little birdy told him, and then he told me." Everyone just stared, not knowing what to think.

Sequel kept a straight face as long as he could. Then out came a loud laugh.

"You should have seen your faces. Your looks were so lost. Lighten up! It is only the fate of the world. We can do this if we do it for us, just us, and all will be fine. Remember, we are only one leaf on the tree of us all, but we are not alone. Enjoy your day; all of Sky Rim can't wait to meet you."

"Don't you think we should go?" asked Supal.

"Don't worry; all things are right on time, don't you think? So come and meet all of your brothers and sisters. There's a lot of them," replied Sequel.

"OK, I would like that. For some reason, I feel like I miss them, and who are these two?" asked Supal, looking to the eagles.

"They are Washi and Kneeoch. Both offer their service in this fight."

"Well, then it looks like we should keep them fed until that time," she said.

"Like I said, leaves on the same tree," he replied. "We all know this, if we listen to our heart," said Sequel. During the night they all enjoyed a great feast, and when morning came, the five, along with two eagles and two horses, started on their way to the next tribe and their gift to help save the world.

Even though they were off to try to save the world, they were still going to live and laugh along the way. It was their life, and no matter what, they would love it because that was what the Warrior would have wanted them to do.

"Where to now?" asked Turak.

"Well, we need to go to the Highlands of Yolk to receive the one they call Two-Chop", said the Blackbird from atop her horse.

"Well then, Two-Chop it is!" said Sequel.

"What do you think about us? Do you think our efforts will be enough?" asked Turak.

"Well, when it was only my father, it was enough, so someone or something is on our side," said Supal.

The way was long and hard as they crossed the river and up into the plateau of the Highlands of Yolk, Yolk being the center of this high plain.

"What is this place? This is like no village I have ever seen. These are not the people I've known to be in our lands," said Turak.

"They're not, as we can see. They are a mix between us and the soldiers, descendants of the two girls who were taken by the ones with eyes of the sky when they were first seen again so long ago. This is a city, as they call it," said Sequel.

"I cannot believe this is real, but my eyes tell me different," said Turak as he tried to take in all that he was seeing. Soon men came to the group.

"You're here; come with us."

The group followed them deep into the city, where they saw many wonders. In the center there stood a round building, and that was where they met Two-Chop for the first time.

"Hello." they were greeted when they entered the place.

"I'm the high clerk of the Yolk. As you can see, we are a people of mixed heritage and hope that you can rest easy in our attempt to not bring harm to any unless under these very circumstances. We offer our champion, Two-Chop, to be our voice to the darkness and opposition of all that is," said the high clerk.

"It is an honor to meet you both," said the Blackbird.

"Well, then do as you see fit, and know that all of our prayers are for you all," said the high clerk as he bowed to them all and was gone.

Then with no more to be said, they left the city and were back on their way to meet another one who had been prepared for them. Now that Two-Chop was part of the group, it was time to start moving back to the people's side of the river.

During this time they all began to understand that even though they were different in many ways, as well as from different places, they were also alike. They all had families that they loved and had hope for the future. Most of all they were all afraid of the unknown.

They were also prepared to give up their lives for the ones they loved. This fight was not only theirs, but also to any that held on to a hope for the future. So, they moved on to the ones that were three, the Girls, as they were known.

The Girls' met the Blackbird at a place on the river, where reeds had been woven together to form homes that floated atop the water. Catwalks that stretched from one home to the next, connecting them all so that a beautiful village held to the surface of the river like a delicate floating flower. Fire flies buzzed around as nets hung out to dry. Canoes were tied to small docks and the smell of fresh fish and crawdads hung in the air all around.

Water tribes were an ancient people that had been formed long ago. They had always depended on the river for their lives, and this was where she met the Girls.

"Hello, I am Supal; what are your names?"

"We are the three that are one, or one in three of the same," they said.

"Sisters only to those who see with their eyes, but to those who see with true eyes, we are all that you are as well." They continued, "The dew of the morning could see that we were life, so where we were it had no need to be. For we were life, and from us came forth a new life. That life was in all. You can call us the Girls or just child. They are all the same."

"Thank you for your people's sacrifice," said Supal.

"Life, when it is truly being lived, is a sacrifice in an attempt to subdue the flesh, having our own will, changing the reality of the seen to reach the higher places in the unseen. It is our honor to be able to witness these last days of the age of now and to welcome the beginning of forever. Now it is as it will be, and the one known as Ten Hands the Spider awaits us," said one of the Girls, who did have in her, the ability of foresight.

"Then here we go. Let us hope we are not late," said Turak.

"There is this time past and the time to come now, so I'm sure we will find him somewhere in between both," said the girls.

Chapter 12

Ten Hands the Spider was the last of his tribe. He had been alone since he witnessed his whole family killed at the hands of the Boneface, the tribe just to the south of his. His tribe was the oldest of the great cave dwellers.

He had sat perched atop the cave's ceiling for as long as he could remember. He had been there since his ladder was knocked out from beneath him as he worked to scrape away the soot that had gathered on the cave ceiling from the many cook fires that dotted the floor far below. The Spider had been held captive by space and time.

The Boneface had attacked the Spider's people as he worked high above on the cave ceiling. During the Boneface rush into the cave, they had knocked his ladder away, trapping him for what seemed like forever. He was trapped between two tie-off rocks, with only a rope to hold on to. He was able to scrape a small ledge out of the top of the cave so that he could sleep, and not much more. A steady diet of bats and insects, as well as hopelessness, was all he had. Looking down on the skeletons of his loved ones made him wonder how this nightmare could have happened. He remembered how they had been before the rats and any number of cave-dwelling crawlers ate their flesh away from their bones.

Most of these days he spent trying to talk himself into cutting himself free so that his nightmare would be over.

"Why are you such a coward?" he would ask himself. No matter how much he wanted to be free, he could not bring himself to do this, and he hated himself for it. He had imagined every way to get down, but not one would work. He was trapped, and he could not die.

Soon a day came when he noticed that his smallest fingers on both hands felt some pain, brought on by maneuvering himself atop the small area that the rope provided, which was the reach of his world. The pain grew, and then he noticed that from the side of his fingers, a small bump did also. After a time it grew to the point he was sure it was an additional finger on both hands. He now had six fingers on both hands. It was not much, but just with that one finger, he was able to reach another part of the cave that he had not been able to reach before. On this part of the cave grew a moss, and on that moss were small snails. So now with the moss and the snails, he might have found a little hope inside. He just stopped to think this was all because he had grown a little finger on his little finger. He had found that he was stronger with six fingers, and he still wanted to die.

Now as more time passed, his thumbs also started to do the same thing the small fingers had. Soon he had two thumbs, a total of seven fingers on each hand. Now a little more was available to him, and with that came new ideas. He wondered why suddenly he had grown these new fingers, but it really did not matter. He was still stuck to the top of the cave with no chance to get down.

Who knew how many seasons it had been. It was like his old life before the top, as he often thought of it, was a dream he once had. If not for the skeletons, he would not have been sure if it had ever really happened. The snails were something he was grateful for, so he decided he would eat them only to treat himself. The moss was also scarce, but he did enjoy it when he could.

He then concluded he was going to move his tie-off rope to another rock. In order to do this, he would need to hang upside-down while he unhooked the anchor, climbing with no rope to the new spot. It would be hard, but at least he had a chance with his new fingers, and if it didn't work and he failed, who would care? At least his nightmare would be over.

So, he planned the details of just how it would be done. He said to himself, "What am I afraid of?" and he did what was about to change his life. He grabbed the anchor, pulling it free. Then, hanging from a rock, he started to climb upside down to the full length of the rope in the direction of the closest wall of the cave. So, then he was a full rope length farther, and his reach was now greater. He could move around more than he had known with his new grip, thanks to the new fingers.

He started to notice that there had not been any light in the cave for many years, but he was able to see. How could this be? He could not understand what was happening to him.

As time passed, his feet also began to grow more toes, just like his hands. Soon he was able to move freely without any need of his ropes, as he found another one that had been left behind long ago by the last person to have scraped the cave ceiling. It had been tucked in a small crevice and out of sight.

Now he had two ropes. With nothing but time, his ropes and himself they started to become one.

Day by day he was moving closer to the walls of the cave. His movement with the ropes became natural as he understood their way, and soon he knew that in time, he would be free. How had this happened? One night he awoke to a small pain in his arm. He reached to where he felt the pain, and something was there. He grabbed it bringing it to his face. It was a spider that had been feeding on him while he slept. He began to understand what was happening. Somehow the spiders were becoming one with him. He then became aware that he had small bites all over his body.

Why now after all this time? What was different? That was when he saw a small snail climbing through the moss. That must have been what it was. Somehow, his new treat turned out to be more than just a treat. It would be the reason he would be free. His mind became fixed on the one thing that would make it all worth it. That would be dead Boneface.

As time passed, he was moving with ease along the top of the cave. The edge was a day away, and he didn't know what it would be like to finally be free. When he finally reached the wall, he grabbed hold of it, climbing down it in no time.

Now only inches from the ground, he stopped to prepare for his first steps in what seemed like forever. He had forgotten how to step down and walk upright. He lowered himself down, and his foot gave under the weight of his body. He fell to the ground, unable to stand. He had been upside down for so long that he could not turn over and feel natural. He was stuck, and all he could do was laugh.

"I'm free now, only to die here without a reason, except that I can't walk." His first night on the ground was not as easy as he had thought. He had been hanging upside down for so long that when it was time to sleep, he made a hammock so that he could sleep upside down. Again he laughed. In time he would learn how to walk upright, though it never gave him the comfort or ease he had when hanging. His backbone had been turned in an unnatural way for so long that walking caused him discomfort. So, he hung whenever it was possible. This is how he became known as the Spider. The name "Ten Hands" came from the speed with which he was able to weave the vines to fashion his web. He seemed to have ten hands, those who witnessed him at work had said.

Now it was time for him to prepare his wrath. He began to fashion his instruments of war so that the Boneface would remember him for the short time they had left on earth. He quickly went to work making the odds a little more in his favor by preparing an announcement to Queen Corona of the Boneface herself.

■ ■ ■

Thousands of Boneface traveled along trade routes by way of the rock canopy. These routes were covered by a petrified canopy of the rock forest for much of the way. Tall trees of an ancient rain forest that had covered the land long ago. This was before they were frozen solid during the Great Freeze. They had been frozen for so long, that once the sun had finally shone, the trees had been turned to solid stone after absorbing the minerals from the ground below.

This is where the Spider would set his trap. He decided that since he was able to see in the dark, it would be the night that he would use to his advantage. He began the journey to the most traveled of all the routes. Once he reached the petrified canopy he waited until dark. The Spider went to work setting the trap. The route was guarded by very few Boneface at night since none of their supplies were being moved during the nighttime hours.

He was able to stay at the top of the canopy as he traveled deep into the Boneface land. Moving swiftly into the heart of them all by way of the rock canopy, high above the heavily traveled trail far below.

The Boneface had no worry of an attack from any foe, especially from one man. This left them unprepared for the type they were about to experience.

Once well into the land, the Spider began weaving the lightweight vine he had brought with him, along with a very sticky sap. He then began placing it overhead, all along the underside of the canopy just above the Boneface heads. When he was ready, it could be dropped down onto them as they traveled during their busy day.

It was a day on which much of the winter supply was being moved from many of the outer tunnels to the inner, deeper ones for their winter storage. Much of it was coming to the surface and being moved along this route.

At the peak time of the day, as thousands of Boneface walked with their loads, one of them noticed a creature high up above them moving about the underside of the canopy. They began pointing and alerting the guards. Once the guards were aware, they began shooting arrows up at him to bring him down. The Spider began leaping around as he held on to the bottom of the canopy, trying to avoid the arrows while finishing the trap.

Once he was done and as the Boneface looked on, he cut loose the net, and all at once, the net fell to the ground on top of them all. They struggled to free themselves from the web's sticky sap, but it was hopeless. Then there was a flash from up above. The Spider held a torch as he yelled down to the trapped Boneface.

"I'm glad you all have lived to see this day—your last day here and you will all know that it is because of me." With those words, he dropped the torch and watched as the web was quickly set ablaze, since the sap was not only very sticky but also extremely flammable. In all, hundreds of Boneface were killed. They had all been burned to ash. This would be the Boneface's first introduction to the one known as the Ten Hands the Spider.

■ ■ ■

A rocky riverbed of jagged stones led to the ancient cave of the first tribe. To travel here was hard, and slow, but the group finally made it to the mouth of the cave, home of the oldest tribe. All but one member had been lost to time. Stale air, cool wind, and bats were all the welcome that the young warriors received. They lit torches and entered the tomb-like cave, not sure where to go.

"Are you sure anybody lives in here?" asked Two-Chop.

"I think so, but you really can't tell by the looks of it."

The group pressed deeper and deeper into the darkness; they could see that the cave was bigger than they had first believed. It gave them the feeling of being in the vast abyss of space. They all had the feeling of being watched when they heard a sound come from somewhere overhead. Every one of them took a moment before looking up to where the sound had come from. As they slowly turned their eyes to the ceiling of the cave, they came face to face with the one known as Ten Hands the Spider. He was hanging upside down, and nobody moved as they all held there breath. The sight of the Spider had every one of them frozen with disbelief. The spider's eyes held an empty gaze that seemed to look past them, locked in a battle between the past and now.

"Hello," Supal finally said, not knowing what to do. "Hello. I'm—"

"The One." The Spider said, finishing her statement. "And I am the Spider" he continued. "If you wonder how I knew it was you, then follow me." The Spider took hold of one of the vines above his head as he started off into the darkness without a torch. He moved swiftly pulling himself through the darkness with powerful arms making it hard for the group to keep up with him.

The warriors could see that just above their heads, the Spider had fashioned a vast web he used to lead them to one of the cave's walls. Painted there were the tribe's stories of creation, all as old as time. He then pointed to a place on the wall where there was an image that was no doubt her, the One. "This is my people's record of all this time of now, as well as the time to come forever. This is how I knew it was you." Said the Spider from somewhere in the darkness above there heads.

They all knew that no matter what, they were right where they needed to be.

"Well, now that you are all here, I would say that our little group is complete," he said.

"I guess it is," she replied, not sure what would be next. On that day until the last day, they never left her side.

CHAPTER 13

The Commander, having seen defeat again and having no way to avenge this, went to a place where only few had gone and from which none had returned. His anger was so great that he could not see clearly what he was doing, and with a vow of his own blood, he sold it away for power, more power than any one man could handle. In that moment he ceased to exist. He was gone, replaced by the one whose name all darkness obeys. He had returned to this time and place with no more dust in his face and without his belly dragging to show all the places he had been—even those very places he was at this moment. It would seem that none would be safe. With this a darkness reached down from above as if to hold all the world prisoner.

It was past high noon, and the Commander was prepared to advance on one of the last entries into the fire and rock below.

As the Commander's army marched, the Thunder Mountains seemed to grow out of the earth, higher and higher, until finally the army's columns stood in the shadow of the sleeping volcano. The men struggled to maintain their pace because of the intense heat coming from below their feet. The ground shifted as they drew closer to the giant plume that rose out of the dark mountain that held the fire deep within.

None of the Commander's men had ever seen the home of the Boneface. The sight of this drew from every man's courage, causing them to struggle even more as they pushed their legs forward. The men hopped over large cracks in the earth that flowed just below the surface with molten lava. The land was barren, with no signs of life as far as the eye could see except for a giant swarm of vultures that circled the skies around the entrance to the Boneface's main tunnel. Then suddenly, the men noticed that off a short way in front of the volcano stood another smaller mountain. It was a pale white, and the soldiers wondered how it could have been overlooked. Then, as if the horror of this ghost mountain was revealing itself to them with a gust, all the soldiers were suddenly gasping for air.

It can't be, the men thought as their minds began to betray them, taking them back to their own childhoods, when dragons and giants filled their nightmares, and the columns for no reason just stopped. The men's legs refused to obey them as they all just stood in disbelief at the sight before them.

"The Tower of the Fallen," a soldier said in a whisper that was heard by every one of the men as a silence came with the disbelief of what they were all seeing.

It was a mountain made from the bones of so many people that one struggled to find the top against the backdrop of white smoke that rose up and out of the volcano. The men could see that the entrance that led into the underground tunnels of the volcano was guarded by only two Boneface. The rest of the landscape was empty. Not even a stone sat atop the ground. Only the mountain of faded bones that had been made at the time of the great storm and during the first March of the Boneface.

"Where is everyone?" one of the men said. Not even a single footprint could be found. The two guards, along with the bones, were the only visible signs that men had been there.

As the Commander's force approached, their boots caused dust to be lifted into the air so that a haze seemed to be surrounding them as they marched. The Commander gave the order to halt the march just a short way from the tunnel's entrance, calling for his messenger.

"Yes, Commander?" the man asked as he stopped, presenting himself so that he could be given his orders. The messenger moved nervously atop his horse, fearing that he would be asked to enter into the Boneface stronghold alone to announce the Commander's arrival.

"Go and inform our neighbors that I wish to speak to their queen," said the Commander.

"Alone, sir?" asked the messenger, his legs shaking noticeably.

"Why not?" the Commander said as he glanced at the large opening that led in to the depths of the Thunder Mountains.

"Commander, it seems it could be dangerous without an escort," replied the messenger.

"Well then take two men, and be about it."

"Two men? That might be a little—" the messenger was starting to say when the Commander spoke over him, amused by the fear that had taken hold of his messenger.

"Men, send an armored escort to accompany my messenger with no less than twenty soldiers."

"Yes, Commander, that should do fine," said the messenger, feeling much more at ease with the escort. Quickly twenty soldiers were sent running to the front to join him.

"Very well, now go." Said the Commander. As the soldiers approached carrying with them the request to the queen, the men could see that the two guards seemed to pay them no attention. Their skin was the color of the landscape, and it seemed that they had been standing there for some time. Their eyes were shut tight, and soon the messenger could see that these guards were no guards at all. These men were chained at the neck to the stone that was the volcano. They did not move, and as the escort began their descent into the underground maze of endless tunnels, the men could see that the tunnel's corridors were lined with Boneface on either side. They had been chained to the walls by their necks. All of these captives appeared to be standing there lifeless with a fine layer of dust on them. They were spaced out shoulder to shoulder, not moving or reacting to the group as they were passed. Long tunnels were lit up with torches that gave off a thick smoke that stuck to the walls turning the space black, covered in the torches soot. The men made their way through the tunnel until they could see that it seemed to open up into a large open space just ahead, and the men marched on. Once the group reached the great chamber, they noticed black faces high on the tunnel walls. There in the center of the open space sat a lone Boneface. He wore a headdress of vultures' feathers and human bones. He held in his right hand a large forked staff that was stained with blood.

"Who dares to enter the hive of Boneface?" the lone man

said as two torches burned on either side of him, and their light was the only thing that was visible. The rest of the area was dark, but the sounds of movement could be heard in that darkness.

"A message to the queen of your people. The Commander has brought his army and requests the attention of queen Corona," reported the messenger, feeling confident with the twenty-man escort. The man on the stone throne remained silent.

"I said, I have a request for your queen," the messenger repeated, looking back on his escort so that he could reassure himself that everything was going to be ok. His tone was bold, almost demanding. That's when the man on the stone throne slammed his staff into the ground. Suddenly, out of the darkness came Boneface warriors. The soldiers attempted to fight them off, but it was of no use. Every soldier was grabbed and pulled to the ground. They were held with their arms and legs pulled open wide, as other Boneface began ripping the armor from there bodies. They screamed, as one by one they were stripped naked. The cannibals then began taking mouthfuls of flesh as they quickly reduced each one of the soldier's to a pile of bloody bones. All the while the messenger stood with his eyes shut tight. His breaths became shallow as he remained still, not wanting to move. He could feel the hot breath of the cannibals on his face.He was hoping to somehow escape the reality of his nightmare when the man on the stone throne stood, slowly walking toward the messenger. The man that wore the head dress slid his tongue across the messengers face, grabbing his head. He attempted to pull away when suddenly one of his eyelids was torn from his face. Again he tried to pull away, but he was held to tight. Then the other eyelid was also torn free, leaving the man's eyes open wide. He found himself alone in the dark space with only the man atop the stone throne, just as before.

"Now run!" was all that was said, causing the wounded man to turn back toward the tunnel as he tried to see through both the darkness and the blood that was now running into his eyes. He stumbled into the tunnel, falling against one of the cannibals that had been chained to the wall. Instantly his eyes opened as the sent of the messengers blood filled the tunnel. His mouth opening and then closing on the messenger's shoulder. He screamed as he pulled himself free, ripping a chunk of his flesh away. This sent him across the space and into another Boneface. Again he was bitten as he pushed the chained mans head away. Two fingers from his hand dropped to the ground and another was swallowed. The messenger stopped in the center of the long corridor to witness the nightmare of his reality. The scent of his blood had caused all the Boneface to open their eyes as they pulled their chains tight. There mouths opening then slamming shut over and over, leaving only a narrow path in the center of the space for the messenger to move through. Down the narrow tunnel the man stumbled as the Boneface continued to take bites from him. Finally, he was seen as he stumbled out of the tunnel and into the sunlight. The Commander watched as the man approached, staggering across the blistering ground and up to the column, his blood leaving a trail in the hard dirt. He stood for only a moment or two before he dropped to the ground dead. He had been bitten so many times in the tunnel that his clothes barely hung on his body. The bones on both his arms could be seen, along with bites from his back and chest.

"Forward!" the Commander shouted as he laughed. His horse as well as the entire force, trampled the messenger's lifeless body. As the soldier's began their descent into the tunnel, they chopped at the chained Boneface. Their heads were left on the ground and the army marched, making their way through the narrow corridors. As they entered the main chamber the men could see the lone Boneface.

"Why are you here? Tell me the reason you have come so far to die when you could have done that at home with your loved ones and without the pain of fire and bone." He said as he sat in the midst of his warriors.

"I am the warlord…" Then his name was said. It was a name that all had known.

"You claim to be who?" asked Roc-mon.

"I do not claim, and I do not repeat myself. Run me through if you think you can, or else bow your heads. Know that who I say I am, I mean."

Roc-mon's face was unmoving. Suddenly his eyes opened wide, and then even wider. He quickly fell to the ground, causing the rest of the tribe to do the same.

"Bow your heads!" Shouted one of the tribe's gifted seers.

"Your father has returned, and with him the Thunder Mountains." Fire and stone had begun to rumble deep within the earth.

The Thunder Mountains had been the home of the Boneface tribe since the Great Storm had caused them to seek shelter in the many tunnels just below the base of the now dormant volcano. It was a land of rock and fire. This land had once been a fertile garden because of the rich volcanic soil, but that was long ago. The Boneface had devoured everything in sight for as far as the eye could see, leaving nothing but a barren wasteland. It was a place where not even thorns had grown since the beginning of the age. They consumed everything in sight. This had happened so long ago that only on the walls inside the great cave could this history be found.

The Spider's people had painted these so long ago, and they were now fading away, just like the memory of his people. The walls told a story of how the Boneface had become so many that the land could not support them. They had hunted and trampled the land until it had nothing left to offer.

As the Great Storm of early on in this age held the tribe's lands in the grasp of a never-ending winter, the winds blew without end. They carried every one of the seeds of every plant away and held them deep within the grasp of their icy hold.

The Boneface, in the midst of this deadly time, chose to consume the flesh of one another. Soon, seeing that without their numbers, they would become the preferred meal of the dire wolves and grizzly bears that now roamed the lands of all the tribes in search of an easy meal.

The Boneface had decided to start making meals of the tribes who lived nearest to them instead. So began the age of the Boneface. The 'March of Fire and Bone' had begun, and it was all told on the cave walls within the Spider's web.

The Boneface lived underground, deep within the now

dormant volcano of the Thunder Mountains. Originally lava tubes that once flowed with the molten lava that formed this land. They had been dug out by the Boneface so that they stretched out in every direction. All of this was under the command of Roc-mon. He was the man who was called on by their queen to uphold her word so that it was law.

Queen Corona was the only one of the tribe who did not have the appearance of skin being stretched over bones. She was a gigantic woman whose appetite was as large as she was. She would spend her days consuming the offerings that were brought to her by her many children as she lay atop a great bed deep within the tunnels of the volcano.

Roc-mon was the father to many of her offspring, all of which were boys, since it was custom to have the females put to death as soon as they were born. Only the women of captured people were kept, so that Queen Corona would be the only female of her royal bloodline.

It is told on the walls deep within the Great Cave that during the time of the Great Storm, there was a day that the storm had come on so fast that in a single moment all who were caught outside were frozen in giant blocks of ice. The cave's paintings showed that nearly all men lost their lives. Very few were not caught in the Great Freeze, as it was known. The few Boneface who did survive had found all the food that they would need for generations to come, feeding on the ones who were trapped in the ice.

Without seeing the sun for so long the children began to believe that it was only a fairy tale that the Queen's servants would tell them to keep them in their beds.

"Go to sleep, or the great fire in the sky will come from out of its sleep and burn you to ash."

This was something that all Boneface had grown up fearing. As the tribe grew, so did the reach of their tunnels, until one day a large stone that led to the land above was dislodged and they once again saw the light of the sun. It would take many years before they would finally come out and once again walk in its rays. They had all feared the light of the sun since childhood, but without any food, they were forced to come out in search of more. A time of terror had begun for all who lived near them. This time was known as the 'March of Fire and Bone'. It was in this time that the Spider's people were all killed. These, as well as many other attacks, would give them enough food to bring them back down below for many more years until now. The Commander's call to them was all the reason they needed to continue their never-ending hunt for human flesh.

"My queen," said Roc-mon as he entered the chamber that she had made into her nest of consumption and lust.

"Yes," she said as she looked him up and then down as if he were a meal that she loved.

"I have news of the most awaited one,"

"Oh, you do. This is most unexpected," she said as she licked her lips, her gaze set on Roc-mon. "Tell me before I burst," she continued as she moaned eagerly.

"My queen, our father has returned."

At these words, a rumble deep within the volcano could be heard. The tunnel walls began to shake, as if to confirm what he had said. The queen's eyes opened wide, as she looked across the chamber to a pile of old bones that had been picked clean. "This news awakens a new hunger in me." she said as she motioned to her servant to fetch her more flesh.

"How do I look?" she said eagerly.

"You look as if chosen by the fire deep within," said Roc-mon as he stood up straight, awaiting his queen's word.

"I do, don't I?" the queen replied as she rolled from her back onto her stomach. Her naked body slick with sweat. "Send word that my sons will move to bring forth our new home. A home of plenty. One that is on the other side of the river flowing."

"Yes, my queen, and what of the most awaited one?"

"Tell him, 'Patience.' Tell him, 'When our new home is taken, then he may look upon his prize. Not a moment before.' I know it will be hard, but all good things do not come first without the price being paid," said the queen.

"Yes my Queen." Said Roc-Mon before disappearing into the darkness deep within the mountain.

The Boneface had called the 'Rock and Fire Forest' of the Thunder Mountains home since the beginning of the age. The Boneface tribe now bowed their knees to the Commander. The Commander had once again sent word to the Blood Disciples, an invitation to discuss a payment owed. A meeting to be held in the shadows of the volcano that suddenly began to rumble without end.

"We have come upon your request," said the Blood Disciple with no name.

"The House of the Blood Disciples have come to ask you who it was that killed our brothers and sister on the other side of the river."

"They were all killed at the hands of the one called the Warrior, and for this a payment is owed," said the Commander. Then he said the amount that was owed. The price was double the price he had paid for the head of the Warrior. He continued, "The reason it is double is that the Warrior's head was not delivered as promised."

The one with no name understood this and was prepared to pay the total amount in blood.

"With this that has been said all being true, I offer the brotherhood of our entire house in full service to you in your mission to destroy the tribes on the other side of the river. To be done until what is owed is paid."

"This payment is an acceptable one; I agree to this," said the Commander.

Once the disciples were added to the Commander's force, they made a request of their own. One among them said, "The tribes are in possession of something that was taken from us. The one known as the Medicine Man once lived by the creed. During this time he stole the Black Scrolls of Assassination and War, written in blood by our brotherhood since the beginning of this age. We are in search of these writings."

"Then let it be known that they will return to you upon our extermination of the tribes." This was to be by the say of the Commander.

The Commander's force was now complete with his soldiers, the dreaded Boneface, and the entire brotherhood of the House of the Blood Disciples. One could not remember a time such a force could be said to roam the earth.

"We have been assembled in the time of now so that when

we march, the very foundations of this world will shake beneath our feet. All shall bow their heads at the very sight of this army so that no man stands before it," said the Commander as all did as he wished and bowed their knees before him.

The Commander stopped seeing his council, and the Boneface were something that the soldiers were not sure of. They never ate, and at night, from inside their tents, a humming sound could be heard. Also, many men a day were sent away, always never to return. They were said to be sent to an outpost. The soldiers were told that the force was to large and some of the men were no longer needed.

"What is this outpost talk, and why are there now too many men? We should need every man, and why don't the Boneface carry supplies, not food or even water. How can a man go without water?" a soldier asked the other soldiers. They all seemed to have the same concerns.

"I think we all know how," said another soldier.

Yes, indeed, they did. These were no men; they were demons, and demons only bowed their knees to one. That one was now the Commander.

The soldiers were wrong though. The Boneface carried all that they needed in both food and blood. That being in the form of soldiers who were sent away to man an outpost that didn't exist.

"We're fighting for our own extinction. What can we do? We need to stop this dreadful army, or all mankind will be food for the feast of demons," said a soldier.

So that was the day that the soldiers awoke to the reality of that time. The day they chose to fight back against a lie.

The men that were taken to man the outpost were always taken in the morning and then held in a place for another day. There were always two days of soldiers being held.

As the men continued to plan a way to somehow stop the Commander, along with the Boneface, a soldier brought word that they would move on a small village by dawn. The Commander had planned to take the land for a staging area, and that would be where their assault on the Warrior's village would begin from.

It was still dark when the army moved out. The soldiers were ordered to hold back as the Boneface began the initial assault. The men quietly crossed the river, surrounding the village without being detected.

The Boneface took the outer huts as one by one the people inside were quietly taken, along with the children, never to be seen again. The bodies of the adults were loaded onto wagons. They were then put into heaps outside the largest tent of the Boneface. That was when the sounds of saws could be heard nonstop, until not one body was left outside. It took most of the night, but every hut was taken without a sound.

As it remained still, the soldiers knew that they had all been killed in their sleep. The army moved on, leaving some Boneface to load the dead back onto wagons. The soldiers were no longer needed to man the outpost. In three more days, another village was to become the next victims of this unholy march.

Soon they came upon a long road that stretched for miles; that was when the soldiers could see just how many the tribe had brought to the fight. An endless wave of Boneface marched across the land, cutting a trail deep into the earth, so that all could see where they had been. Soon the beasts had been eaten and replaced by the Boneface. They made long lines that were tied to the war machines. With the Boneface's combined effort, the machines were pulled along the path the ones ahead of them had carved into the earth. It seemed there was no end to them all.

"March," yelled one of the soldiers as he continued to push the pace of the march.

"Commander, my men are requesting to stop for a moment," said one of the Blood Disciples.

"Why is that?" replied the Commander.

"We've been marching most of the day without rest."

"And what is the problem."

"There is no problem; it's just that my men are not soldiers and are not use to traveling at this pace."

"Roc-mon, are your men in need of rest?"

"No, Commander."

"So, there you have it, the Boneface are not soldiers and they have no problem traveling at this pace."

"Yes, but the Boneface are, um…"

"Are what? Speak your mind if you have something worth saying," the Commander said as he moved his hand so that it rested on the handle of his sword.

The disciple with no name thought for a moment.

"Nothing, Commander, my men are just being soft."

"I do believe that; now fall back in with your men. Leave your horse up here with me, and show them how it should be," ordered the Commander. The Commander's second in command, as well as Roc-mon, watched as the disciple with no name got off his horse and joined his men marching with the others.

"We move on another village by morning," the Commander announced to his second in command.

"Commander, my scouts have informed me that the village has very few men. They seem to be all farmers and gatherers. Mostly women and children. They are no threat and will only slow us down."

"Yes, but it won't take long to put them where they need to be," said Roc-mon as he slowly opened his mouth wide, so that his bloodstained teeth could be seen before he slammed it back shut. His stare became intense as he looked the soldier in his eyes, letting his gaze follow the soldier's body down to his feet, then back up to his head.

"What's wrong? You seem frightened," said Roc-mon.

"Maybe it's you and your warriors who are frightened. That is why you would waste your time on this village."

Roc-mon took a step closer to the soldier, stretching his body until he was so close that his hot breath could be felt by the soldier.

"My warriors know no fear. If your men cannot do this, then what do we need them for? The Blackbird has already received word of our arrival by now. She will no doubt be prepared. So what does time matter now? Maybe it is your men whose stomachs battle causes to turn."

"My men have no problem with battle, but they are soldiers—to slaughter women and children for no reason except to entertain themselves is not what they are trained to do. What honor is there in this?

"Does the cat not entertain himself with the mouse before he makes a meal of it?" Roc-mon answered as he stepped even closer to the soldier, causing the soldier to place his hand on his sward. With the men standing face-to-face, neither man was willing to look away.

"We do not make meals of the dead," replied the soldier.

"Boneface love the taste of the fallen. If you could do this, then the fear that you hold on to would leave you, and you would know that there is only one thing to fear in this life— that is Boneface!" Roc-mon continued. "It does not matter if you don't know this already. You and your men will soon."

"My men have no fight with you Boneface."

"No, but you will. Does the wolf make friends with the rabbit? No, he does not. Boneface are the wolf, and your men are the rabbit."

"Enough! The only fight we have is with the tribes, for now. The two of you, as well as your men, may find out who is what, once we are done with the tribes. Whether it be a wolf or a rabbit, we will all see," the Commander said as he also stood, his hand once again resting on his sword. Both men instantly broke away from each other's stares.

As the group of young warriors started their long journey home, the Blackbird noticed that the Spider was looking her way.

"What is it that you are thinking?" she asked.

"I'm just trying to make sense of this all," he said.

"So many have died, and even more will, for what?" asked the Spider.

"That is the problem with war: one can make no sense of it. Can I ask you something?" said Supal.

"I know what you want to know. You want to know about your father."

"Yes, you spent more time with him then almost anybody. I just wanted to know what he was like."

"He was easy to understand but hard to explain. He didn't speak, so we had to learn how to communicate, but it wasn't hard. He would express himself with his whole being so that there was no mistaking what he was saying."

"So what did he tell you? Can you please tell me something, anything, about him."

"He was not much different than anyone else, except that he was like no one you've ever met or will ever meet. He didn't see what the reason was that so many should die, but he knew no other reason to be, except for what he was created for. That is why he had come that summer to this side of the river. He thought that if enough men died, then war would end, so that there would finally be peace. Once the summer was over and once even more had been killed, he realized that it would not stop war from coming. He just wanted to return home to his people. He was tired and only hoped that our fight would carry on without him, so that this wouldn't all be for nothing. He hoped that one day our brother would join him, along with Turtle, in the home of *us* all. Once he did this, he finally went to a place he had always wanted to be. I believe Turtle was there, and his pain finally stopped. Who your father was and who he became were not his choice, but what he did with it was. Your father was robbed of the life everyone else had, the things he had witnessed them all enjoy, but he also realized once he was given the chance to live their lives in the village, he just couldn't do it. Battle was where he first felt alive, and he realized without it the rest of life would be even worse than being alone. To consider the others when none had considered him was something that he would not burden himself with. The ones he had always wanted to be accepted by had become his burden. He couldn't do any more than he had done for them. He realized that he would never find his smile, so he stopped looking, and he was fine with this. He lived his life for Turtle and for battle. Battle was his smile, and that was something he could only share with the ones he had sent home to the next. Those men were all ghosts. That's why he was the Warrior. This is something that I almost understand, though not fully, like your father did. In the time that I had spent alone stuck to the top of the cave, I learned more about who I was. That's something I am grateful for. Your father also knew these things. He had lived his whole life alone, and that is why I believe he understood even more than me. Your father had already found the way to what lies on the other side, and he was not afraid. He had not lived his life here but in the next. This is where his home was. Your father knew that he could never truly be missed here because no one really knew who he was. They had only seen what he had done, but he never could express to them how he was. Without a voice he was never heard, therefore never really known. He had already lived our fears in this life so that he truly could welcome the next when it came to take him by the hand and welcome him home. He was just a visitor here, only wanting to say he was here. He wanted us to know that he would see us all in the next so that he could properly welcome us home. That is who I believe your father was."

Those words still on her mind, they continued to where this journey had begun. As they did, they were all united in one thing: stopping the Commander from taking more than he already had. After many days the group finally reached the people's lands and soon the village. They were all welcomed home, and smiles appeared on the faces of all. The Blackbird sat with her people; what she heard next was almost more than she was able to understand. An army led by the warlord had destroyed one of the villages in the far south. All were killed, but a trapper had seen it from a treetop where he hid. The things that he saw were never to be spoken of again, but know that they would break the hearts of even the heartless. The Blackbird had sent scouts, but without any word back, the army could only be thought to be coming to finish the Commander's unfinished business with the people.

"So now we have heard the news of the southern tribe, lost to war, and we shall not wait to give this enemy our answer. For we are few, but in us is something mighty! It seems this foe has mistaken us for those who would not fight, and this is their mistake. We have prepared our answer for them, and that one is true. So now we draw a line. Hear my request, Two-Chop, Ten Hands the Spider, Sequel with the Rim Clouds, and Turak—go to the path that is narrow but high. There make them know that our people will fight them every step of the way."

■ ■ ■

When the warriors arrived at the pass that was narrow and high, the Spider began pulling large vines across it at different heights. Then he began covering them in a very sticky sap. One could not loosen its grip quickly or easily. Vine after vine he tied with the skill of a real spider. He placed them so that no one could pass without being caught in this web of delay and vulnerability.

Two-Chop cut large logs as Turak placed them in rows in certain places so that when ready they could be cut loose and allowed to come rolling down across the road over all who stood in their path.

■ ■ ■

Reaching the narrow path that was cut into the side of the cliffs, the Boneface led the force with the soldiers in the rear. The war machines were too large for them to be moved through the pass. They would need to put them onto rafts and use the river to make their way down until they found a spot that would be wide enough to unload. The soldiers oversaw the loading of the war machines so that the force would be divided in two.

The Boneface flooded into the pass, and they seemed without end. One after the other, they set foot on the narrow road. They soon came to the place where the web had begun. The disciple known as the Crypt, of whom it was said to meet him in battle was to welcome death itself, unsheathed his blade and tried to cut the vine down. It gave, and instead of cutting, his blade became stuck in the sticky sap. As he pulled to free it, the vine stuck to his shoulder and held strong. He reached with his free hand. It too was stuck. Then he tried to roll away using all his strength. His whole body was then trapped. As the others looked on, they saw that behind him was what looked to be a pair of eyes entangled in the web.

"What is that?" one of the men asked.

All their attention was now on the stare of the web.

"What is it?" yelled the Crypt as he struggled to free himself.

The eyes moved slowly toward the entangled disciple as the others moved back.

Their eyes were on the creature inside the web.

"Don't leave me!" shouted the disciple as sweat ran down his face. "I'll kill you all! Don't leave me here!" the stuck man shouted as he could feel someone or something moving closer to him. Then came the sound of fluid spilling on the ground as the Crypt's eyes opened wide and set themselves into a blank stare. The others looked on as a puddle of blood formed beneath the dead man as he stood upright, held by the web.

"Did you see that?" one of the disciples yelled.

"What was that?"

■ ■ ■

"What is the delay?" the Commander shouted, still sitting atop his horse.

"It's some sort of web that cuts us off. It's spread over the trail as far as can be seen."

"A web? What do you mean, a web?" the Commander shifted his weight, becoming restless.

"I'm not sure, but that is the word from the front," replied one of the disciples.

"Cut it down, and be done with it," said the Commander.

"They say it cannot be cut. Already, our brother the Crypt is dead,"

"Dead? How?" asked the Commander.

"A creature of some sort calls the web home. It killed him as he was held by it.

"The Spider," Roc-mon said. The Spider was a bitter enemy of the Boneface. The mention of his name caused an instant uneasiness among them all. Roc-mon continued speaking. "If it is the Spider and the web extends as far as can be seen, then there is no hope. We must turn back and go by way of the river."

"Why would we do that?" asked the Commander.

"Because it will be impossible to pass. The Spider will be in the midst of the web, able to move freely, and his blades will see us all dead before we can make it through to the other side. So there is no hope."

"What about burning it?"

"The sap burns for days, and the vine does not. It will take the rest of this season to burn. All the while, the Spider will take us one by one. We must turn back."

It seemed all the Boneface agreed.

Just then, as the Commander considered this, he heard a loud rumble and screams. Two large trees had been cut loose by Two-Chop. They came rolling down like the feet of giants over ants, crushing all the Boneface as well as some disciples who stood on the narrow path. As soon as this happened, another pair followed with the same results. The trail was torn from the mountain, creating large gaps that cut off the Boneface and disciples alike from the main force. As they looked on, Sequel appeared from across the trail and with his bow began shooting the trapped men. Sky Rim eagles appeared just above these men. One by one they were pulled from where they stood and dropped to their deaths by the eagles.

Without cover and with no where to hide, the men began grabbing hold of one another as they attempted to shield themselves with each other's bodies. As they did, the men started to unsheathe their blades, trying to fight each other off so that they would not be used as human shields. This would only prolong the inevitable.

Soon, the men in their panic did not even notice that Sequel was no longer shooting his arrows at them.

Sequel sat back and watched as the last two men danced with each other on the narrow ledge, fully engulfed in a bitter knife fight for their lives, thrusting their blades with the intent to kill one another every time their blows were offered.

Finally, one of the men was caught, pinned to the mountain with nowhere to go. Just as the blade of the other man was driven into the trapped man's neck, a Sky Rim eagle picked up the remaining man by the back of one of his legs and pulled him to the sky. His eyes looking straight down as the ground fell away, further, and further so that the men on the ground below appeared to him as if they were ants. The man could only pray to any of the gods who could hear his prayers, but the prayers seemed to fall on deaf ears, as he was dropped and rushed back to the ground. He spent the last moments of his life remembering those he loved, and even though he would never hear the Warrior's words, they were certainly true because in those memories he knew that he would be missed.

A tear fell, dropping to the ground just ahead of him. It marked the very spot his head would hit along with the rest of him. The main force could only look on and be grateful it was not them. That would be for only a moment, as Turak began dropping large rocks down on the heads of the Boneface from the cliffs above. Man after man was crushed in front of the others.

"Retreat!" they all shouted. It would be to the river, and the Commander's hate for the tribe grew with every step.

As the warriors started back from the path that was narrow and high, the Spider could see that both Two-Chop and Turak seemed to walk with a glazed look in their eyes. Both boys were quiet. Their expressions were blank, and they seemed to be somewhere else as their heads hung low on their shoulders, their hands trembling.

"What's wrong with you two?" the Spider said, his eyes on both of them.

"Nothing," they said at the same time, both boys stopping to look at one another.

"Now you're starting to sound like the boys from the Wolf," said the Spider as he took a step in front of them both, blocking the way.

"What's going on?" Sequel asked as if he had not been paying attention.

"I'm just checking on the boys here," replied the Spider.

"You two OK?" he asked again. This time his stare into their eyes was hard, and the two knew he would not let up without an answer, both knowing exactly what he was asking but both afraid to say it.

"Go ahead," Two-Chop said to Turak, motioning with his head to speak on what it was that both boys had on their mind.

"No, you can. I'm not much for too many words at once," replied Turak, his eyes indicating he desperately wanted the subject to be forgotten.

"Well, one of you say something—we're losing daylight, and it's going to be said before we take another step, so let it out." The Spider had begun to attach a vine to the nearest tree as Sequel found a nice patch of grass in the shade to sit down on; he could tell that they were going to be there for a while. Both eagles were flying high above in large circles. Still both boys stood silently, neither one wanting to say what it was that kept them so quiet.

"I know what it is," said the Spider as he was just finishing up with the other end of the vine. He had begun to pull himself up so that he was hanging there upside down looking both boys in the face.

"It's OK to feel what you're feeling; you wouldn't be human if you didn't," he continued. "I know it's not easy, and that's why what we are doing is so hard."

"But why is it so hard?" Turak asked with an almost-cry, like that from a young child for his mother when the child has become lost. Desperate to find her. The sound of her voice the only thing that will calm him.

"Yes, why is it so hard?" Two-Chop was also looking for the answer to the very same question.

"First say it, say what it is that is hard; say it, and then your answer will come," said Ten Hands. His face remained still, the sunlight casting his shadow on the ground below him.

"I don't think I can," said Two-Chop.

"I don't think I can either," Turak said in agreement.

Both boys were standing with their shoulders slumped downward.

"You need to if you want this pain to loosen its grip on your hearts. I'm not saying it will go away, but it will be at least somewhat understood," replied the Spider.

"OK, that would be something at least," said Turak.

"Why does it hurt so much to…"

"Go ahead," said the Spider, his face unchanging, his eyes blank. Both boys noticed this blank stare at the same time. It was a look neither one could remember ever seeing.

"To…to kill a man," shouted Two-Chop as tears came from his eyes.

Turak seeing this, let his head fall into his hands as his tears also came. Both young warriors were overcome by the memory of just a short time before.

"I didn't want to kill those men," said Turak as he tried to regain himself.

"I just wanted them to stop, but they wouldn't; they would have never stopped," said Turak.

"When I was a boy, I remember my grandmother had told all us children the stories of war," said Two-Chop. "She told us of the sickness and what it does to men."

"I didn't want to kill them either, but he's right. They cannot see what is true, but still, even knowing this, it hurt. Their families are in their homes waiting on them. And what of them? Only to become food for the beast, never to be heard from again. All because I killed them. I know it had to be done, but it still hurts. I just wish I could tell them all that I truly am sorry for taking their lives, that's all."

"Yes, I feel the same; I'm sorry to them, as well as their families, who will miss them," Turak said as he wiped his eyes and straightened his back.

"They know," said Sequel as he stood up and walked over to the young warriors.

"How do you know?" asked Turak

"I am from the Rim Cloud companions of the light. In this place there is a gate, and behind that gate is all that is true. I have walked through that gate, but it was not in this time. Know that what I say to you I have seen. All things there beyond that gate are known. Just as you have spoken to us, you also have spoken to those that it was meant for. That is how I know, so look forward to that day when you two will pass through that gate, and then you will also be home. Thank those men, for we all will see the day when our brother will once again join us in this fight. Remember, not even one will be forgotten," said Sequel. With those words the four of them moved on.

Chapter 15

The soldiers were destroying the last of the war machines so that they could never be used against any of the people. "I hope she is who they say she is" said one of the men.

"Who" asked the man beside him.

"The Blackbird," the soldier said.

"I hope so too" said another soldier, having overheard the conversation.

The men knowing that the same words echoed in all their heads. "who's a wolf and who's the rabbit?"

Some of the men's heads started to nod knowing that she had once been their enemy, but now she would be the hope they all held on to.

"Come on, men. Let's move. The Blackbird awaits our company!" shouted a soldier. Her name alone drove them to beyond their own limits.

"For the Blackbird!" they shouted, and their feet seemed to have wings.

■ ■ ■

Word came from a scout that had been sent to keep an eye on both the Boneface and the Commander.

"The Commander and his force are returning. The Blackbird's warriors have stopped them at the pass. Many were killed, so it will be the river they will be traveling. They are moving quickly and are not far behind."

"What can we do? The war machines have all been destroyed, and there are too few rafts for us all," said one of the soldiers.

"We can let as many men as can fit on the rafts go ahead and warn the tribes. The ones who stay can say that we too fell under attack and we are all that remain."

"What choice do we have?" The soldiers knew that there was little time and they had to decide quickly.

"Who goes, and who stays?" another one of the men asked.

It was a hard choice to make as every man wanted to never again be in the presence of the Commander or the Boneface.

"Well, what's most important is that the Commander does not win. The ones who can help the Blackbird the most would be the ones who should go first." The rest all agreed.

"Since the horses are with the Commander on the pass, it should be the men who ride heavy horses that stay."

It was true. What good was a horseman without a horse? It was settled.

Two brothers who came from a small village, this being the first adventure that they would share in their young lives together, said goodbye to each other. One being a horseman, and the other an archer.

"It's OK, brother. We'll see each other soon," the oldest brother said as tears filled his eyes. He continued to reassure his younger brother of the things he was saying. This would tear at the hearts of all the men because they all knew that it was very possible that it was not true.

■ ■ ■

When the Commander heard this news, his hatred was even more than ever. He began to thirst for the blood of the tribes like never before. With no rafts and no way to go by way of the pass, it would take some time to build more. Meanwhile the Commander and the disciple with no name and Roc-mon gathered to speak of what would be next.

"Our men seem to be spooked. None talk as they sit around their cook fires. Their spirits are not good; I feel many are considering leaving our cause."

"Yes, I agree," said the disciple.

"Then this must be corrected. Each of you assemble your men, and I will do the same. Bring them to the center of the camp, and we will show them what will happen if any should choose to abandon our cause."

The two did as they were told, and the attention of the entire force was brought to witness what would be the punishment for desertion.

"Make no mistake" said the commander. Looking over the entire force, he continued. "This will be you if you do not remain with our cause. Bring me a man" he ordered, looking to Roc-mon and the Blood Disciple. Both stepping to the men who were gathered around the Commander. They were all close so that they could hear what he had to say, and that was when a soldier was grabbed. The man began to shout, "No!

What are you doing?" as he looked desperately into the eyes of all who were around, hoping to catch someone's look of sympathy, someone who would help him fight himself free. As he did this, all the men who stood nearest to him began to look to their toes. Losing the ability to understand his words. This was especially hard for the soldiers to watch. They had grabbed the older brother of the young archer who had left on the rafts only hours before. He had reassured his brother that they would see each other soon, so they could continue their first great adventure in a lengthy line of many.

The man was tied to a stake and lifted into the air. The stake was then set above a fire that blazed, and he was cooked. His screams could be heard even after he was dead, imprinted into their heads for days to follow. When he was charred black, the Boneface ate his flesh until only his bones remained. Then two others were killed in the same way. After this, none would consider anything but what they were told.

■ ■ ■

The soldiers who went by way of the rafts were making good time, as they were eager to put as much distance between themselves and the dark army they had once been a part of. They had hoped their fellow soldiers would be able to convince the Commander of the story they had told. Soon they came to the place where they would leave the river and continue their march to where the village was. The high mountain pass would be all they needed to travel. As they marched, across the trail there stood sixteen dire wolves. Their teeth showing as they growled, snarling viciously. Suddenly the twins appeared standing with the pack.

"Why have you come?" As they spoke these words, they looked to the ground. Dug out of the trail was a line set in stones. The soldiers could see that the boys from the wolf held long blades in both hands.

"Speak now of your intentions," said both twins at once.

"We come in an offer of brotherhood and to take up your fight. There is a dark army that marches to you as we speak. Their intentions we do not agree with. We have come in great sorrow for all we have done to your people," said the soldiers.

"Then you may pass, and it is *our* people. Welcome home, know that while you were gone, you were missed," said the twins as they stepped aside to allow the soldiers to pass. "Know that we are one with all who love." The boys said, and

in the soldiers' faces, they knew that this was the truth. Once they reached the village the soldiers told of all they knew. That was when the Blackbird asked a question. "Do you want to fight? Know that nothing is expected of you. If you choose to fight, it should be for *us*. If you do this, no matter how it ends, it ends. Hate wins, and we die, or the love wins in us. Only we will remain and everything else is left behind."

With that and all at once, they all raised their hands and shouted, "For us!"

They were all ready to defend the people from any harm that was meant for them, and nothing else mattered. It was in good timing because a traveler had come through the village. He spoke to the people, telling them of things he had seen. He claimed that the warlord of their past was no more than one day's journey to the south. With him were the Blood Disciples, along with the entire Boneface tribe. They were many in number and directed to the village.

"They intend to take your harvest, as well as put your men and old people to the sword. They are planning to make an outpost to serve advancing armies into the land. Your strong women are to be put to the fields as slaves, and the young children as well. Their arrival should be soon."

With this news a strong feeling of dread came over the village. A mumble began to grow among the people. Then an old woman spoke to them in a loud but caring voice. "Look, all of you, let your eyes see that she is here. With her is the spirit of our people. Her father is here with us now. He sees us in this, our darkest hour." The way the woman spoke caused a familiar feeling to come rushing back, reminding them all of the Warrior.

"For our children and our home, remember what he did for us. That is what I say to you. You see her now as a girl in the midst of soldiers, but she has already sent word to the crow. The buzzards have already been given notice. Tomorrow the table will be set for them all. Her father will dance with her, and that dance will be written in the blood of all who hold hate in their hearts—the dance of the Blackbird. So hold your heads up so that they may see you from the treetops. Remember that she is no longer just a girl; she is the Warrior returned. Our enemies will remember that this is the peoples home." Those words caused a great weight to be released from them all. The Commander would know why he had not already been there.

It was cold, and the soldiers breath was in the air all around the camp. They huddled around their cook fires. Many of them lost in their own thoughts, remembering the savagery of the night before. It would forever be inside their heads. The soldiers could see as the disciples walked from tent to tent of the Boneface, but none ever came to the soldiers. What was the reason for this? The Boneface were all coming out of their tents, only to stand in the night air. There glances told the soldiers that something was wrong. The men all exchanged looks as they pulled their weapons close to their sides.

"What's going on?" one of the soldiers asked as tent after tent of the Boneface were emptied. All holding their weapons. Their looks were serious, as if they were preparing for something sinister. Not one disciple approached the soldiers. Feelings of uneasiness grew, causing a soldier to walk from fire to fire.

"Prepare yourselves" was all he said as he quickly moved to the next.

The soldiers knuckles were white as they gripped their weapons.

"Be ready" a soldier yelled.

Without warning, the night was set ablaze. Small clay pots of pitch and oil were flung in the direction of the men. Balls of fire burst everywhere, causing panic filled screams to break the silence. Men began to run in every direction. Dark smoke surrounded them all. The ones that were able to find their way out met the Boneface and their spears. Boneface cries of battle were mixed with the soldiers' screams.

The disciples were atop a hill that overlooked the scene of terror. It wasn't long before every soldier was dead. The

Commander knew that if the soldiers had been attacked, then where were the bodies of the dead men? Not one dead soldier could be found. So it was again that the Boneface feasted on dead soldiers.

The next morning, the rafts were ready, and the Commander sent his men and supplies aboard and prepared to move down the river. Man after man they went. One after the other set out on the river to their final show of power. Soon all under the sun would be claimed as theirs—only theirs and no other.

The Commander was the last man to be seen that morning. Most of the rafts were already floating downriver. As he came out from his tent, he was not in his usual armor, the one that showed his familiar crest of the lion and sword. Instead he wore armor of blood red with a black crest bearing the dragon. In its right hand was a child and in its left, the child's mother. All the while it sat atop the world. His helmet was adorned with the horns of a ram. As soon as the men had seen him, all fell to their knees as he carried the mace known as the Morning Star—a war club of kings' past. It was said to be the right hand of the Dark Lord himself. How the Commander came to possess this as well as the armor, none knew. They bowed their knees, and not one dared to look at him. All knew that the Morning Star had a thirst like no other. A thirst that could only be satisfied with blood.

"The force has begun the march. They have orders to await you at the pass that leads into the valley of the tribe." said the disciple, who for the first time in his life knew what fear was.

"Very well. What of my horse?" the Commander said. He

seemed to already know the answer to the question he had asked.

"Your horse—oh yes, your horse is on its way downriver as well. He awaits your arrival," replied the disciple as sweat began to fall from his face.

"Oh no, that will not do. I mean to take another." Then he looked to his right, and out of the earth came forth a steed as black as all nights. The warhorse of ash and smoke.

"He will do," he said as he turned his attention back to the disciple.

"One more question—what is it that you think of this?" He held the Morning Star above his head.

"It is magnificent," said the disciple. He could not take his eyes off the weapon. He had never wanted something so badly.

"Yes, but it has a thirst, and I must take heed to this thirst, do you understand?"

As these words fell on the disciple's ears, so did the mace, killing him at once. No man dared look, and only the black warhorse came forward. As the Commander took his place atop the unholy beast, he began the descent to join the army who awaited him for the final part of the march. One that would end with the extermination of the people.

As he floated down the river, he thought of the Warrior and of the Blackbird. By this time the next day, the people would all be dead. With that, all this known world would be his. What would they say at that moment when all hope was lost? Would they beg? Would they scream, or would they try to stand tall, as he hoped they would? Then all would see he was absolute above all who would stand against him.

CHAPTER 16

The battlefield was known by some, but for others this would be their first taste of war. The young warriors would meet the entire Boneface tribe, as well as the House of the Blood Disciples' entire brotherhood. They now marched under the banner of the dragon that would rule the world. Once at the spot where the Commander would exit the river still atop his horse, ready for one more matter. Then it would be the tribe's last, so the Commander stood before his army.

"Blood Disciples," said the Commander. All the Boneface looked on. "Come to my feet, and when you do, know that your brother is dead by my hand." He then slowly raised the Morning Star into the air, still dripping blood from the work it had just done a brief time before.

"If any of you have anything to say, say it now. If not, then bow your heads to me!" the Commander shouted.

The disciples all came forward by their own will and strength to show power and pride for their house.

"Do you have anything to say, or will you bow your heads to me now?" asked the Commander.

The disciples thought for a moment, and then one by one, they all bowed down to the one who stood before them, the Commander. As the Commander looked over these men, and as the last man bowed his head, the Morning Star also did. Smashing a disciple's head, killing him at once. When this happened, and as the disciple's heads were still down, the Boneface attacked, giving them no chance to defend themselves. Within moments the disciples all lay dead. "Throw these cowards into the river! Let the fish have their fill of them," ordered the Commander.

Now the Commander was ready to turn his full attention to the people. "Boneface, forward to the village," he ordered.

As they marched, not one would tire. The Boneface traveled with their queen as well as all the children of their tribe. Queen Corona sat atop a platform made of bones that had been taken from servants who had once served her. It was a constant reminder of their fate. The servants had the unfortunate task of carrying her platform on their shoulders the entire way to their new home. The queen in the middle of all her warriors, the children at the very back without anyone to look after them. The smallest children, the ones who could not defend themselves from the older children, were killed as soon as the eyes of the queen's servants were turned away from their care.

"What is taking so long? We should have been there days ago!" said the queen. "It is much too hot for my delicate skin. Stop there in the shade so that I may cool myself and have something to eat," she continued with a more than demanding tone in her voice.

"My queen, our father returned has ordered the men to continue with the march. He asks that the queen's guard stay behind and the main force continue. He assures you that it will be safe."

"I see that he is in a rush to view his prize. None would blame him for this," said the queen as she took a bite out of a dead man's arm, stuffing her mouth full. Barely chewing it before stuffing more of the arm in her already full mouth.

"Tell him it is OK, I praise him for his discipline. He must be going mad with lust for my royal treatment," she said as she rubbed herself all over her giant body. It was only for a moment as she soon tired, shoving more flesh into her mouth.

"Stop here and make camp. Have my servant come so that he may please me," said the queen.

"My queen, we shouldn't allow the main force to get too far away," said the guard who oversaw the rest.

"And why not? You heard your father returned. We are in no danger" she said.

"Yes my queen, forgive my foolishness," the guard said. Suddenly a vine dropped from somewhere above him in the tree that he stood under, hitting his shoulders. The guard looked up to see Ten Hands the Spider riding the vine down head first. His blade held out in front of him so that it hit its mark, cutting into the guards face and through his neck. He was left gasping, as the Spider came to within inches of the ground. The queen's guards rushed to protect her but it was of no use. The guards had made a mistake they would live to regret. The Spider sprung up, and back into the tree as spears came flying from every direction.

The guards looking to the treetops when suddenly a muffled gasp could be heard. The Boneface all turned back to see their queen atop her platform with the Spider sitting on her giant shoulders. He quickly wrapped a vine around her neck, pulling it tight. Her mouth was still stuffed with a dead man's flesh and she struggled to take in air. The guards rushed to help but the Spider had already begun climbing back up and into the tree. He pulled the giant woman up with him. Higher and higher she rose just out of reach of her guards. Her arms waving back and forth, as she desperatly tried to free herself. She was left hanging for only a moment. Her weight was too much, causing her eyes bulged as the veins in her face could be seen beneath her skin. A loud crack came next and her head was pulled from her body, falling to the ground. The guards stood in disbelief, looking at one another as the children came in a great swarm. Hunger driving them so that they shoved their faces into the open wound. The guards attempted to stop them when suddenly one was pulled to the ground, and eaten by the young Boneface. The guards all stepped back to watch a plump young girl climb to the top of the queen. She fought off the rest of the children so that she would have her fill first. Only after this had happened were the rest allowed to take their place to consume what was left. It seemed a new queen had taken the old one's place.

■ ■ ■

The army of the Commander traveled the last part of the pass, knowing they would be at the village soon. The Commander sitting atop his horse when Roc-mon seen a shadow far off in the distance. "A wolf Commander."

The Commander replied with doubt that this could be true. "No, it couldn't be," he said.

"No? Why do you say this? The dire are known to hunt in this land."

"They were the only thing that my men were able to get their blades into the last time I came this way. Total extermination of the pack. Sixty-two full-grown wolves were taken so that must have been your mind playing tricks on you in the cold."

"Are you sure, Commander? It looked like a wolf," said Roc-mon.

"You question my say? Man, run ahead and show this fool that what I say is so."

With this, a Boneface ran ahead to where he was told. When he came to the place where he had been sent to check, he turned to signal them that there were no wolves. Suddenly a large black wolf appeared out of a shadow, pulling the Boneface to the ground. This wolf had once served a man but had been freed by the Warrior long ago.

"It's only one wolf. That man was enough to feed him for a day or two," said the Commander. One wolf turned out to be sixteen, all with a taste for men. The wolves knowing that these men meant to bring the people harm had taken so many men from hiding places just off the trail and in plain sight. It would be a long night for the force as they marched.

■ ■ ■

As the young warriors remembered all they had seen, they returned to the village. All were eager to hear what had happened on the pass.

"It's good to see all of you have returned," said Supal.

"What is it that you have to tell us?"

The young warriors seeing that many soldiers were among the people were not so eager to say. Then the Spider stepped forward.

"My words are—" he started to say as he tied a vine to a nearby tree, and then ran it across to the next one. He spoke as he did this. "I am full of joy to see all the new faces…" He paused, pulling himself onto the vine. He let himself relax as he hung upside down, resting his sore bones after the long journey. "It saddens me to say that the rest of the soldiers are dead."

"Yes," said Sequel. "All of the soldiers that remained are dead."

"What of my brother?" asked the young archer.

The others had heard what the warriors had said, and it was doubtful that any of the men would have been spared.

Sequel stepped forward and said, "I'm sorry to say, but not even one soldier was spared."

The boy could not help himself, and the tears began to fall from his eyes.

"What of his body? Did they eat my brother?"

That was when the Spider answered, "No, the men fought their way to the river. They were unable to find the shore because of the many Boneface arrows. They all were drowned and swept away by the river. Not even one was made a meal of."

"Thank you for that, but I know that is not true. My brother was the best swimmer I have ever known. The river flowed calmly, and if he had made it to the river, he would still be alive," said the brother of the dead soldier.

The rest of the surviving men were without words. They did not want to know any more than they had been told.

"Sorry for your loss. For our loss. Gather around, and hear my words," said Supal.

The men all moved closer.

"My father came to the very place that we are now. The night before battle, and he was also in great pain. He did not know any of his people, nor did they know him." Supal continued, "I think that he must have felt like a single star amid all the sky, alone and afraid. My father did not sleep on this night. No, he waited on the sun and on the moment he would answer those who took what he loved. He waited because that was all he could do, a star among a sky of darkness, and he did not sleep. He would not sleep until he let those and all who were there know that his friend Turtle was loved. Even if by no one else but him. Then he would show them all that was more than enough. His love was worth more than all their hate because it was his. He wanted everyone to know that Turtle was loved. Love does not die. We do, but love lives on. So when we step on the battlefield remember us all. Know that if you leave us, you will be missed. Know that where you go, we also are. Always there in these moments in forever. So know this, and your fear will be gone, replaced by our love." Supal explained. "Hold true to this fight. This is our home, and we will defend it, even at the cost of our very lives. If you should leave this place on this day, know that I will see you in the next. We are one, and one we will remain forever."

The men all thought of these words and started to nod their heads in agreement. Not one slept, not even one. All prepared for the next day, to show all that war had no place anymore here in this time. So they waited.

They took their positions on the battlefield. All eyes were on them, and with that all the hope of the people. They were sure that no one had ever felt so alive as they did at that moment. All fear had gone; there was only the anticipation of the drums so that she could dance.

She stood before forever; she heard the voice of the unknown deep within her heart. These are the words she heard:

"Many have come to this place; all have failed. What makes you believe that you will not also fail?" The Blackbird replied, "I know I cannot win, but I must try. If I fail, I know I tried. Without that I will have nothing. I could never have lived my life only to die for nothing. When I stand before the Creator I can honestly say, that I have nothing, but I died trying.' That is how much I loved this life that he gave me. Hopefully when this battle is over, it will return the people to who we are. To the ways of our ancestors, the ways of the people. A moment is remembered forever, so we will make this and all the rest count."

At her words, the voice within said, "If you believe that you cannot win, then all you have to do is give him what he wants!"

"What he wants? What is that?" Supal asked herself.

"What we all want. If you listen to your heart, then you will know."

As she thought of all that she had heard, the world seemed to again stand still. Then it was time.

■ ■ ■

The Commander took the field. His armor showed bright red with the black dragon that sat atop the world. The black horse of ash and smoke tore up the earth. It's eyes shone as red as the armor the Commander wore, a warhorse who himself had taken the lives of many men. Its muscles bulged beneath his pure black coat.

The Blackbird knew that this would decide the fate of all. She sat atop the white spirit horse of swift judgment, riding the length of the field as all eyes fell upon her. Her hair blowing in the wind of the spirit horse's powerful strides. Her eyes were all that could be seen, their gaze never leaving the Commander. The black warhorse rose up as a scream came from out of its soulless heart. The call was answered by the spirit horse as it too reared up. All at once they both charged the middle of the field, gaining speed until they were at a full run. Each trying to go faster than the other. The Commanders weapon held high over his head. The Blackbird with nothing but hope. The Commander took a swing as he passed, and the Blackbird was thrown to the ground by the power of that swing.

As she stared up into the sky, the Commander dropped down from his horse, standing over her.

"Stand," he said.

Her body was in pain from the fall. She slowly pulled herself to her feet to face him.

"Now bow your head to me. If you do this, I will spare half of your people so that they may serve me. If you do not, then love dies with you all," said the Commander as he gripped the morning star.

"That is something that I will never do," answered the Blackbird.

"Then you all will die," replied the Commander as he slowly walked closer to the girl.

"Do you have no pride in yourself so that you would let all see that you are a fool? Your name to be remembered forever as one? Why is this so hard for you to see?"

The army of the Commander, as well as all the people looked on. It was clear that the Blackbird would not win this fight. She could feel her strength leave her body.

The twin boys of the Wolf tried to help her, both rushing in with everything they had, but their blows were easily blocked.

"Do you mean to kill flies? You cause a great pain in my side from the laughter that your effort brings," said the Commander. Then it was his turn. He swung his weapon like a young man in his prime. Both boys having not the ability to defend themselves were easily killed.

"The drummers!" shouted the Commander. The drums were quickly made silent by the Boneface arrows. The Blackbird looked to the sky, and as she did, she was grabbed by her neck and pulled into the air. At that moment all hope was lost.

"Bring me some chains!" ordered the Commander. She was then chained and bound and put to the stake, a trophy displayed for all to see. Next the people were taken. The men and old ones were all put to the sword. The women and children were then caged in large pits until they were to be worked, all under the watch of the Boneface.

"So they say you are the one. The one what?" the Commander asked. "How about the one who will never be free again, the one who will serve me for the rest of her days? The one whose flesh will be eaten by beast or burned by fire, so that your screams will rise into the heavens. A song to the gods of war sent on my behalf, a tune sung by the One. Their consideration for me will be great, all because of your screams. Thank you young one. I cannot wait, but for now I will," he said.

This was more than she could take, and she thought how foolish she had been to believe she could win. *Now look at what has become of your people—all because you believed a lie.* She was now made a spectacle for all to see, shamed and in great sorrow. The cries of the women and children were constant, and she was no exception. She cried day and night. She could hear the Commander's voice ordering the Boneface, "Take this spot here and dig a ditch so that the water can flow inland under the oak trees. Cut them all down and use the lumber to build an outpost. Make places to house the slaves as well as the beast. I expect this all to be done by the new moon. Start on the fields as well so that we may harvest and work them all from sunup to sundown. If they drop, kill them on the spot for all to see, the Blackbird most of all. If she does not look, then kill two, and make sure one is always a child. If they rise back up, kill them anyway. We have too little food, so it will matter not. We must lessen them all by half. If you run out of food, then feed them grubs. The riverbank has plenty.

"We will be moving farther into the land in two days, and I expect to hear the whips cracking until sundown every day until the work is all done."

"Yes, Commander, make no worry of this," replied one of his men.

And it was so that there was hardly a moment that the sound of the whips was not heard from that day on.

"Move, you useless mites!" the Boneface shouted.

The Boneface could be heard nonstop, and as the people fell, they were killed on the very spot. The ones nearest to them were then to throw the dead into the river. Soon the people were only half of what they had been. With no more children, that meant the end of the people. They would be no more as the ones who still lived died. All of this under the watchful eye of the Boneface.

The Blackbird was set atop a perch in the center of them all, chained high above without even shelter. The weeks turned to months, and the sun baked her skin until it was as black as coal. The cold turned her toes the same so that she could no longer stand. Her hair dropped from her head, or the birds tore it from her scalp as she slept. It was all she could do to keep them from doing the same to her eyes. It seemed she never found rest as the Boneface made wagers on their ability to throw small round stones at her and hit their mark. Then one day one of their throws was true, hitting her in the face. She was left with a bad wound to her eye. Without care it soon became infected, and then both eyes. Finally both were lost to the infection. She was now blind. All the while she sat atop her perch, and she wished that she had never been born. At least the tears had stopped, and still she had no way to die. The few women who were left had only grubs to eat, or starvation would be there to welcome them into the grave.

The Boneface found them to be attractive since they looked as if skeletons had come to life. Soon they began to lie with the women, and children came of this. The boys were raised to be slave masters and the girls' slaves like their mothers. All the while the commander traveled further into the land making slaves of all he seen. Soon the outpost had grown into a small town and then a large one. A town that was built on the backs of women whose families had been butchered by the Boneface. It was said that if all the tears that had fallen there had all fallen at once, they would have made a mighty river. Upon the Commander's return to the town, he would always make sure that the Blackbird was unchained and brought down. She was given the greatest of care before being placed back upon her perch so that she would live to hear what had become of her people.

Then she awoke. She couldn't catch her breath as she remembered the horrible nightmare.

"It was a terrible dream!" She said to herself as tears fell, and she knew it was more than just a dream. It was what was to be if she and the young warriors did not defeat the Commander. She was to not only save her people but all the people in this world that they all called home.

The fight would be to much for her, and she feared that she could not win even with the help of the others. So the night before the battle was to take place, she went to the only place she knew she might find help. To the center of the village and her father.

CHAPTER 17

The air was cold as a slight breeze blew through the leaves, making a hissing noise that disturbed the calmness of the night. Tears ran down Supal's face as she said these words in the form of a prayer. "Father, I know that I am your daughter, but I don't know that I can do what is being asked of me. I'm afraid, and that is why I am here. If you truly see me now, then please hear my words.

"Fear has taken hold of me. I feel all will be lost unless your courage finds me on this night. The same night that also found you."

As she sat waiting on an answer, the tears continued to fall. She felt her body weaken with all her worry being more than she could take. She lay her head down there on the Warrior's resting place, finding sleep.

The next morning she awoke to a man she did not know. He wore turtle shells over all his body. He held in his hands a spear and an ax. She was frightened at first, but when she looked into his eyes, she saw that they were kind.

"Who are you?" she asked.

"I am the one they call the Warrior, but I am also your father."

"No, that can't be—" she started to say, but at that moment she could see someone familiar in him.

"How can this be?" she said, not believing what she was hearing. "How did this happen?" She said as she stood up slowly to face him.

"My heart beats again because of my people's—" And then he stopped. "*Our* people's love," the Warrior said. Then she remembered all the Medicine Man's writings as well as the stories that the old ones had told.

"It was your words and your tears I felt, and it's your love I've become."

The next moment she ran to him to receive a much-needed hug. She could recall everything she had been told.

The people's love had been branded over his heart so that even if his heart could beat no more, it would beat for him. So it was the night before battle and the Warrior had returned. One by one the people awoke to a wonderful surprise.

An old man was heard saying, "I told you he'd be back. I touched that very seal myself, and that's how I knew I'd see him again."

To the younger people's surprise, almost all the old people agreed.

"That's him! Just look at him. I helped cut and shape that armor myself." Indeed he had in his youth done just that. One by one, just like before, the old ones came to welcome him back. He was happy to see the ones he recognized, as well as the ones that he did not, and it felt like home.

The old ones along with the rest of the people felt the reunion alike, but it was short-lived. Suddenly a rumble could be heard, and the old ones quickly recognized it as being the sound of an army marching. As the army approached, the ground shook causing a wave of animals of every kind to come rushing into the village as they attempted to flee the approaching horde of Boneface. Bear and deer among other types of forest dwellers came charging out of the forest just ahead of the Commander. There were so many animals that the people were forced to take shelter or risk being trampled .

The Warrior looked at Supal. "Do not let fear overtake you!"

"How can I not? If I lose, then everything I love dies," she said to her father, looking for some sort of help.

"Don't fight so that the people will not die. Everyone will die someday, but fight so that you can live. Fight so that you are seen and not only seen but remembered, so that when you are gone, the memory of your love for your people will live on. When you do this, then you are truly living and helping those who you face in battle also live, for in their last moments, they will know that they all will be missed. The ones you help find rest for the last time today will be the proof that you lived.

"I never lived until the day I first stepped onto the battlefield. I was never seen before that day. Once I was in battle, I was not only seen by all. I was also known by all. So when you do this very thing, be grateful to these ones for helping you live, and send them to the Creator in joy that they will be home because you lived." Then again she woke from her sleep.

The Blackbird sat atop her white horse. Then she saw her people looking at her with hope and love. The men of her tribe all took a step forward. That was when a hunter spoke.

"I know that we are not warriors, but we are all that we can offer. We want to fight for our home."

"Bring up your bows, and let your arrows be the rain that will fill the sky, so that our enemy will be touched by your hand. To those who chop wood, bring your axes so that you may cut down our enemy." The ones who carried axes stepped forward.

Then her horse rose up and made a call to his own. From out of the forest came horses running to the men. As they passed, the men grabbed hold of their manes pulling themselves up onto their backs. The Blackbird began mixing ash with water and a small amount of honey, making a black paste. She then smeared it on the face of one of the hunters. "Why do you fight?" She asked.

"To protect all that we love, and for us." Answered the hunter.

The Blackbird shook her head at this saying, "You are wrong. You are all warriors!"

The morning air was cold, and the Blackbird thought of the ones who were there with her then. They all sat in silence looking straight at the field that would soon welcome them all to shed blood and prepare a feast for the black swarms. As she sat staring into nowhere, she knew that she must hold back the rage she felt inside. She felt forced and robbed, but most of all, she felt alone. She felt this because of one man—the Commander. It was because of him her father was dead. It was because of him these young men and these girls would bow their heads, and take death by the hand.

The young warriors all looked to her. Her eyes met each of theirs. She thought how incredibly brave they had been, and continued to be. Even now in the face of the Commander, and the entire Boneface tribe. Seeing that they all stood tall in defiance of this army. Even if there was no reason to think that they could win this fight, still they all believed that they would defeat the Commanders army. They believed this because of her, because of who she was. She was the Warrior's daughter. If the Warrior could do those things he did, all for the love of a turtle. They believed that she would also do the same for the love of them all.

They all understood what the Commander did not. When the warrior stepped on to the battlefield for the first time it made him feel so alive. To know that he might be seen, not by the people but by turtle filled him with something he had never felt before. He knew his reward could be found in battle and for the first time he had hope for the future. That hope was now in the Blackbird.

"Prepare, Boneface, for your day of payment is overdue. The blood that will be spilled today will be your own. These words are written in stone."

With that, the grips on the stone knives and axes were tightening as they looked across the field at the ones who would soon feel them.

"Return our brother, or not one of you will leave this field alive," shouted the Blackbird.

"I think it is you who will not leave alive," yelled the Commander.

"You dare bring your army against me!"

"I brought no army, they are my people," said the Blackbird as she held back the rage she was feeling.

"These ones are not worthy to be soldiers," said the

Commander as he looked to the young warriors. "These boys are the least of my worries. My army is more than any of you could ever hope to be."

"That is because they are not soldiers; they are my people, and they would never put their hope into something so meaningless as armies, war, or murder. Our hope is for the things that are unknown to you or anyone like you. They earn no wage by your blood; they are warriors who fight so that not only them but you as well will know that they lived. But for a moment, and in that moment, everything is left behind— something you will see as you try to hold on for one more."

"What of the Black Scrolls?" asked the Commander.

"Those writings are at your feet. Never to be known again. Only those who stand before you know their teachings, and they will die with them. We are one in the teachings of love taught by a turtle and now felt by you. You will know that you are the only one that will not be missed."

Then the Commander looked to his feet, seeing ashes that were once the Black Scrolls.

"My horse!" shouted the Commander; now all eyes were on him. "You think that your people can stand before me?"

"No, I stand against you. You're a memory and a dance my father showed me," she said. With this, her hand rose, and the drums began.

As powerful drums shook the sky, they sang a song of birds, and in that song was an invitation to the black swarms.

"Come and feast, for the Blackbird has set the table."

Suddenly the call of a lone raven could be heard as it sat atop an old tree. Then another one from another tree's branches.

Just like before the trees of the forest started to sway up and down. Dark birds filled their branches, yelling as if they were shouting a warning to all that death would be served shortly.

The Boneface, thirsty for blood, began to buzz in a near frenzy of lust for the young warriors' lives.

"Easy!" shouted the Commander. "Soon," he said.

The Boneface could not hold back their eagerness. Rocmon shouted, "Leave none standing! Cut them down, and leave them beneath your feet! You will not live to see your seed grow. I promise you that."

Suddenly the sky seemed to hold to itself, holding its breath as frost started to form on the trees branches; suddenly the calls of so many others came on like a rush of noise that assaulted the morning, violently shaking them all until their attention was had. All who were there turned their heads to the sky, their eyes open wide. A great swarm started to form above the village, the giant flock swirling around in a large funnel in the skies around them. From inside the swarm, they could see vultures circling even higher in the sky as they formed another swarm high above the first one, the red of their bald heads glistening as they looked down to the battlefield, knowing that the table was about to be set.

The soldiers ran to the front.

"Shield wall!" yelled a soldier. Instantly the men formed a wall with their heavy shields. These men had prepared for this day, and their eyes met as they braced for the Boneface's rush. The Boneface had killed their fellow soldiers, and every man was ready to return to them what they were owed.

"Long spears on the ready!"

The long spears took their position behind the men holding the shields, spears drawn back and ready to thrust forward. The spearmen held the spears gently in their hands so that their grip on them would not be stressed when it was time to let the Boneface feel them.

"Steady, men; remember your fallen brothers," shouted a soldier, all the men's minds recalling the broken promise of an older brother.

"Archers, set! Loose on my command."

The archers stabbed plenty of their arrows into the ground next to them as they strung one on their bow. Their hands were steady; they pulled back an arrow in one motion, holding it a moment before slowly letting their arms relax.

Next the people's hunters lined up on either side of the shield wall atop their horses. Every horse held a hunter and an axman. The young warriors took their place in the front of the shield wall, with the Blackbird in the very front of them all.

The Commander, atop his black warhorse, started laughing so loud that his voice echoed through the whole valley. He looked at the people's answer, and then he raised his hand to the sky and made a fist. As soon as he did, a wave of Boneface with slings that held the clay pots of oil ran forward, their slings twirling around in large circles. All at once they were flung into the air, and the lit fuses could be seen against the early-morning sky, made dark by the swirling funnel that lurked silently above them.

"Loose!" yelled a soldier.

At his command, both the soldiers and the hunters let the rain fall as their arrows took to the sky. Both the pots and the arrows arrived over the center of the field at the same time. Pot after pot broke into pieces as the soldiers', as well as the hunters', arrows were on their mark. When the few remaining pots did land, the fires were easily put out.

Then it was the Blackbird's turn. She thought of the intent that the Boneface had with the balls of fire that they had let fly. Her anger was what she needed, and she was off, running straight for the Boneface with the slings all alone. She leaped from one leg to the other with the beat of the drums. The Boneface could not believe what she was doing, so they hesitated for only a moment, but it was a moment too long. The beat held them in a trance so that their reaction was slowed just enough that they could not take hold of their blades before she was on them. Only a few bow-lengths away, she jumped into the air, spinning as she took another stride and then another as she rose higher and higher until she was well over their heads. Then as she passed over them and their eyes were on her, she turned around in the air so that they were facing each other, and that was when from out of her hands came flying so many quills that there was no hope. Every Boneface was hit with many of them. All were forced deep into their flesh, and the tree frogs' poison did the rest. Before she hit the ground, they were all dead. Once her feet touched the ground, she spun around to face the Commander's army, and as she did, many more quills came flying straight at the Boneface, dropping many more of them to the ground dead. Every step was to the beat of the drums. She spun and then jumped into the air, and as she did, the quills never stopped coming. As she hit the ground, she crouched with her downward momentum pressing her body flat to the ground as Boneface arrows came rushing just over her head, narrowly missing her. Suddenly she was up again as she sidestepped a Boneface, leaving quills pushed deep into his rib cage, dropping him dead no more than a step or two behind her.

All the eyes of the Boneface were on her. None of them noticed that all the hunters on horseback were charging at full speed straight for them. The horses plowed the Boneface down, the axmen chopping at any who were near as they passed by. Again the arrows of the soldiers took to the sky. Boneface dropped as they were hit. The shield wall started to walk forward at a steady march. The hunters' horses passed through the Boneface, and the hunters jumped down, letting the axmen take hold of their horses as they strung their arrows and let the Boneface feel them. More and more Boneface dropped as the horses charged back into them.

The twins, along with Turak, Sequel, Two-Chop, and the Spider, rushed what was left of the Boneface front line. The ax men on horseback came plowing from the rear. Many Boneface had already fallen by the time the horses met up with the warriors in the middle of it all. The Boneface who still stood were tripping over their own dead as they tried to join the fight. This delayed them long enough for the axmen to pick up the warriors on their way back through the Commander's men.

The Blackbird was picked up by her white spirit horse as well , and they all returned to the safety of the shield wall just as another wave of Boneface slammed into it. "Hold the line!" yelled a soldier. "Push!" And the men all pushed forward with their shields, driving the Boneface back. "Long spear!" And the spears were thrust over the shoulders of the men with the heavy shields. Boneface were hit in their chests as they were impaled by the spears. They were pulled back into the wall of the front line, when the spears were brought back so that another blow could be given. Another push, and the Boneface were again met with the long spears. "Archers." The soldier gave the command, and arrows came flying just over the other shoulder of the men holding the shields, hitting more Boneface in their heads, dropping them dead where they stood. Another push, and the soldiers could feel the bodies of the dead Boneface under their feet. Other men with short spears sifted through the fallen Boneface, stabbing them through their black hearts. The hunters let loose one more volley of arrows before running into the forest at the edge of the field. Some Boneface tried to give chase, but as they entered the trees, they were met by the wolves, who had been waiting on them. They were torn to pieces and so gave up on trying to catch the hunters. They only hoped to make it back to the field.

Next were the drums, along with the Girls. The Girls took their place next to the drummers as they unwrapped a crystal drum that was covered in rabbit fur. It was placed in the center of the eight drummers, along with the Girls. Next the women ran out to hand all the fighters' pieces of beeswax to place in their ears. They put it into the ears of the ones who held the shield wall for them. Then it began, the drums being hit in loud rhythms. That was when the one who spoke in the ancient language that had been heard through the Great Storm began. She looked into the crystal drum, and out of her mouth came a voice that was so beautiful tears came to the people's eyes, and then it came on louder and louder until the crystal drum hummed. The sound got so loud that one could not even hear one's own thoughts. Soon the Boneface started to drop to the ground as the pain was more than they could handle. As this happened, the soldiers continued with their push, walking at a steady pace as both the long spears and archers continued to mow down so many Boneface that soon they were walking on a road that was paved in the bodies of the dead.

Next the girl who had dominion over the small and many called to them all. Worms came up from the earth and started eating at the flesh of the Boneface as they rolled on the ground in pain. The wasps and bees came next, stinging them all over, and finally the ants came to pick the flesh from their bones. The Commander, seeing that his men were near defeat, began to shout orders. The Boneface started to gather up a rage inside of them that was fueled at the sight of so many of their dead. They were preparing for another rush when out onto the open field walked a plump little girl with the scent of a queen on her. She opened her mouth and called to what was left of her warriors. "Boneface, to me!" she yelled.

The Commander tried to shout above her, but the Boneface paid him no attention. They all quickly gathered at her feet. Then the child said, "I want to go home, back to the Thunder Mountains, home of my mother and her mother before her."

The warriors then picked her up above their heads and began to carry her home. As they did this, she looked to Roc-mon and waved her hand in front of her face. "To ous satu pish," the words of her people's past. With those words, the warriors fell upon him, consuming his flesh in one quick swarm, leaving his bones in the dirt as they passed.

When it was over, only the Commander was left. He sat atop the warhorse of ash and smoke, his once mighty army destroyed. As he looked about the field, the Boneface remains were scattered everywhere. The black warhorse reared up on its hind legs and screamed as if all the ones who had lost their lives to it had shouted at once from a place somewhere deep inside it. The Blackbird's white horse also reared up to answer the challenge. It was the dream she had had all over again. Both horses charged to the center of the field at once. The Commander swung the mace with intent, but Supal had jumped from the back of her horse and was well above the reach of the Commander.

As he rode past, he pulled with all his might on the reins of his horse so that it would slow. He did this as he turned the horse so that he was now facing her. She stood there alone, her eyes wide open, among the dead Boneface. As the Commander stepped down from his horse to face the Blackbird, she dropped her weapons and took up a blade of grass, a single blade of grass, and then she began the dance.

As she did, the Commander shouted, "You come at me with a blade of grass?"

"Yes, it is, but it's also my home. Something you want so bad. You will have it, but that is all you will have. The rest is for the people, the ones who know that this place can never be owned. The time for words is over!" the Blackbird said as a calmness swept over her.

From behind his back came a heavily armored hand, and

in it was the mace known as the Morning Star. He moved his arm as if he could barely gather the strength to pull his weapon across the damp ground. Then, without thought, he fired it straight for the head of the Blackbird, meaning to kill her in that instant and prove to them all that her hope was nothing more than childish dreams. In his mind's eye, she fell limp to the earth. All marveled at the effortless skill he had shown, but this was only in his mind because the next moment, he felt the flutter of a blade of grass tickle the tip of his nose and then the back of his neck. He swung violently around, driving his mace home, but found only air. Then again the tip of his nose tickled, and there was a flutter in front of his eyes to blind him. Again he swung the Morning Star, finding only air. In his blurred vision, he thought that he had seen a girl and then a crow, but it was only a blade of grass. She touched him at will, knowing that had she wished it, any one of these could have taken his life.

The soldiers looked on in a sort of pity, and in that moment, he knew that all his effort was for nothing. Then he heard a humming in his ears and a laugh. He was overtaken with rage, and then she appeared before him without weapon or worry. As his hate overtook him, he lunged forward, not having the focus to notice that he had stepped beyond the cliff on which they fought, and in his rush, he was carried over. He turned and reached out as if to find a handle in the air, but all he found was a blade of grass, a single blade of grass. He was being held above space by only her fingertips, and in that moment, their eyes met. It was as if his whole life had been lived in that single moment. Then she let go and turned back to all who watched. As she looked at both the soldiers and her people, she raised her hands to the sky.

The sign of her people's love, the sign of *us*, was branded into one hand. In the other hand, she held the hand of the Commander, washed clean by what it was he wanted, what we all want, and that is forgiveness through true love for another. She chose to love him in that moment. She chose to do this so he would return to us all. He who fell away was all his hate, and that one, they did not know. Then both the people as well as the soldiers also raised their hands to the sky, and not one ever thought to look and see where the one who had fallen, fell.

All eyes were on the ones who remained. It was just the two of them, as our brother was returned to us all. In that moment they were who they were always meant to be. The sky opened, and the glory of us was there for all to see. As the scales fell from his eyes, he remembered what he had forgotten so long ago and replaced with hate. In that moment he realized that this story was about him. It had always been about him.

Then as this happened, the ground began to rumble, and there was a loud explosion. Off in the distance, a huge plume of smoke could be seen filling the sky. Rocks were falling from above, everywhere, as the Thunder Mountains erupted. The people of the land of rock and thorn were running from their homes. Lava rushed into the towns as the people all ran to the river. Once they were there, they remembered all that they had done to the tribes. The people were there waiting to meet them. The Blackbird stood high as she rode atop the white horse. She waved a flag some of the children had made for her. It was a bright yellow, with the image of an oak tree on it.

The branches were twisted and bent to form the image of the people's love, the sign of *us*, along with a blade of grass. This was the signal that the rest had been waiting on. As the people from both sides of the river looked on one another, the lava came closer and closer.

The people from the land of rock and thorns did not know what to do, and then to their surprise, the tribes started calling them over. "Hurry!" they shouted as they threw ropes over for the others to take hold of. Everyone was saved, and not even one was lost. After many years the land on the other side of the river was replenished, and so began the start of a new age.

"This was completed in the time of thunder, steel, and armor. Then he looked up, and as he did, he felt his body start to fade away. His spirit rose to join the light, and all were happy to see him. They hugged him and reintroduced themselves to him, and it felt like home. This was as it always should be, right. Then they looked back down to the world and watched you. Then one by one they all started to raise their hands so that they could come down and be with you, so that not even one would be forgotten. Return to your first love, and everything else will be left behind.

"That is how the people found Eden. That is where they still are today. Our life is only a moment in forever. What we do in those moments is remembered, held in time by the Creator so that everything is known. Every time and everything are open for all to see. So in these moments, in this time, Supal found what they were all looking for: their brother, who had been lost but now was found. She remembered to listen to her own heart so that she was reminded that we all are the most important person to the Creator. For this, we all tip our hats to you, young one, and say thank you for living your life not for yourself but for another. It was great, and everyone was there. All this is so that not even one will be forgotten.

"You see, Benjamin, we can all be the greatest warrior in someone's story if we love them enough. A little love is a lot stronger than a lot of hate. If you have the courage to love, then you will live forever. Even after you are gone, your memory takes on a life of its own. That is how we can return to the ways of our ancestors, the ways of all as they were known to *us*."

The End